Secrets

Secrets

Thelma Morrison

briston house
TORONTO

Copyright © 2003 by Thelma Morrison

All rights reserved. No part of this publication may be reproduced or transmitted in any form or by any means, electronic or mechanical, including photocopying or any information storage and retrieval system without a licence from Access Copyright, 1 Yonge Street, Suite 1900, Toronto, Ontario, Canada, M5E 1E5

National Library of Canada Cataloguing
in Publication Data

Morrison, Thelma
Secrets

ISBN 1-894921-10-0

I. Title

HM8712.C4M87   2003
364.78'9   C2003-988450-7

Printed and bound in Canada.

Typeset using Book Antiqua and Monotype Corsiva (main text) and Garamond Classic Book (chapter headers)

For those who helped

Secrets

I

"Janus was the god of departure and return."
– New Larousse Encyclopedia of Mythology

The blood of the great Italian artist Caneletto ran in Jenny Canal's veins.

Those would be the same veins that her husband seemed to think she was opening. Over him.

As if.

In fact, Jenny was trying to open the safe in their bedroom. Her husband, Bram Lockhart, didn't think she knew it even existed. But she did. She also had the combination. She'd come across it years ago and kept it for future reference.

Well, the future was now. What had no future was their marriage. Just half an hour ago, Jenny had come home unexpectedly early from the gallery and found Bram in bed – in their bed – with Shay Walker.

Shay! Real name, Cheryl. The gallery's resident airhead who could, on her good days, be trusted to answer the phone. Usually. She was also 25 years younger than Bram.

Good God.

For once, Jenny's hot Italian temper didn't overwhelm her. Instead, an icy calm descended as she looked at the tangle of sheets and sweaty bodies.

"Shay, get out of here!" Jenny said coldly. "Bram, I'll be in the kitchen."

But once in the kitchen, her bravado deserted her and she felt sick and shaky. Dear God, Bram and Shay! It had to be a dream, maybe a bad joke.

But it wasn't.

A moment later, she heard Bram's car start and Jenny listened, amazed. Bram let Shay drive his precious Mercedes? Jenny had never even been behind the wheel! Her indignation swept away the sick feeling, just in time, as Bram entered the kitchen.

"Now, Jenny, before you get all upset, just listen, okay?" Bram said. "Let me explain."

"Explain? The situation is pretty clear. All you need to know is I'm outta here."

Jenny marched back to the bedroom, locking the door behind her. She didn't even look at the touseled bed. Instead she dug the combination out of her lingerie drawer and began trying to open the safe. Bram was hammering at the door.

There! Open. The first thing she came across was a porn magazine, its cover featuring a naked girl on her knees in front of a man performing fellatio. Jenny snorted and cast it aside. Typical. Under the magazine was a plastic bag containing five piles of $10,000 each. Jenny hesitated, then scooped up two of them.

Just then, the door crashed open and Bram fell into the room. He seemed bent on rescuing her and stopped in confusion when he saw what was really happening.

"Hey, wait, that's my money! You can't do that!"

"Oh, yes I can!"

Bram grabbed her wrist. Jenny pulled away and took a

deep breath.

"You have a choice, Bram. You can let me take this $20,000 and never have to give me another cent—or I'll hire a crack lawyer and take half of everything."

Bram looked shaken.

"Everything?" he repeated stupidly. "Look, can't we talk about this? One little mistake and you're calling it quits? Taking my money?"

Jenny saw red.

"First of all, I wouldn't exactly call it one little mistake. Second, it's not your money, it's our's. Now, get out of my way!"

Defeated, Bram moved aside and Jenny swept through the doorway. She didn't pack a thing. Let him keep it all, she thought furiously. Sheer momentum took her through the house, into her old Datsun and down the street. When she got to the plaza at the corner, however, reaction set in. Hurriedly, she parked the car.

Then she had a complete nervous breakdown. Oh God, oh God, how could he DO this? I love him. NO, I hate him. Bastard! Jerk! Prick! What am I going to do?

Ecetera.

When the storm had passed, Jenny dried her eyes and drove calmly out of the parking lot. She knew exactly what she was going to do. A few minutes later, she turned north on Airport Road.

Next stop: Wasaga Beach.

II

"Janus was first the god of all doorways."
– New Larousse Encyclopedia of Mythology

Two hours later, Jenny felt the tight band in her chest ease as she turned onto Shore Lane. Visiting Aunt Janetta at Wasaga Beach had always made her feel good, forget all her worries.

Of course, Aunt Janetta wouldn't be there this time. She had died two months ago, leaving her property at Wasaga Beach to Jennie. Bram's eyes had widened with glee as he realized they now owned 150 feet of prime beachfront land. He'd had a For Sale sign on it the next day. Jenny had protested feebly, but Bram had overwhelmed her with logic. Summer was their busiest time at the gallery; they would never use the place. Best to sell it, create a little nest egg.

However, it hadn't sold yet. Waterfront land like Aunt Janetta's came with a prime price tag. It took time to find the right buyer. And Jenny had decided to hide out in Wasaga Beach until that person came along.

Jenny grinned as the huge carved head came into view a couple of blocks away. Aunt Janetta had had it made years ago and it was now a landmark. Janus, the Roman god of two faces, looking ahead, looking back. It wasn't an especially appropriate name for a cottage court on Nottawasaga Bay, but Jenny's aunt had never let details like that stand in her way. The name reflected her Italian heritage and exemplified her outlook on life, she always said. So, Janus it was! And he was, after all, the god of arrivals and departures — there was plenty of that at a waterfront resort.

Until ten years ago, Janus had been a bustling cottage court, full every summer with families and every winter with skiers. Then, at the age of seventy, Janetta had said enough and closed the place down. She didn't rent out the cottages any more, but she had continued to live in her beautiful old house on the bay. That's where Jenny was headed now. She would stay in Aunt Janetta's house for a few weeks until she figured out what to do with the rest of her life, how to live without Bram and the goddamn gallery; how to live without goddamn Bram. And the sale, when it came, would finance those plans. Janus was the one thing in the whole world that was all her's. Bram had no claim to any of it.

Jenny turned the car into the drive, passing through the tall cedar hedge that had always given Janus its air of another world, protected, enclosed. A world where nothing could go wrong. Janus was magic, always had been, and Jenny felt better just turning into the driveway.

Jenny caught her breath as she pulled the car to a halt. Janetta had never wanted cars as part of her special world, so the drive ended near the back of property. Ahead, between there and the house, stretched the famous Janus garden, filled with Roman statues, Apollo, Aphrodite, the Three Graces. And bursting with spring: tulips, daffodils, hyacinths, grape hyacinths. A dusting of forget-me-nots, thousands of them, lent a drifting, blue glaze to the display. Aunt Janetta had been a stellar gardener and even after her death, what she had created lived on. Jenny felt her neck prickle at the thought, then grinned to herself. Of course, she thought. Aunt Janetta would have seen to that!

The garden looked in good shape, considering its recent neglect, Jenny thought vaguely as she leaped out of the car and headed up the garden path. Even the path looked freshly swept. Then she swallowed hard as she caught sight of her aunt's prized mock cherry tree.

"That tree is the most beautiful sight in the whole world—for 15 minutes each year," Aunt Janetta used to declare ruefully. "Then the wind comes up and poof, just like that, its blossoms disappear!"

But not yet, Jenny realized. Its spring blooms were still a tightly-curled secret, giving only a pink hint of the glory to come. Jenny felt a rush of pleasure as she realized the tree would bloom in a couple of days.

And I'll be here to see it! One last time, she thought. Aunt Janetta would be pleased.

Jenny let herself in through the back door and made her way down the small, dark hall. She ignored the doors that led to the kitchen, the bedrooms, heading straight as she always had for the living room. When she reached it, she groaned with sheer pleasure.

The great glory of Aunt Janetta's house had always been its huge front window, running the whole width of the house, just as the living room did inside. "One of the great windows of the western world!" Aunt Janetta used to declare. When Jenny, as a child, once asked why this sweeping statement was confined to the western world, Aunt Janetta had smiled wryly.

"Alliteration," she said.

But it surely was beautiful! The whole panorama of the bay filled the window, water and more water, a heartbreaking blue, edged with a ribbon of sand, the misty Blue Mountains forming a dramatic backdrop. Jenny stepped closer to the window to follow with her eyes the curve of the beach. "The longest freshwater beach in the world," Aunt Janetta used to boast and, indeed, the stretching sands curved right out of sight. A full nine miles, Jenny remembered now; you could walk forever and not come to the end of this natural phenomenon.

Jenny caught sight of her aunt's old field glasses resting on a small table, just where they'd always been, and she laughed with pleasure, snatching them up at once. Early morning herons, gulls, terns, passing boats, the ski runs on the mountain—Aunt Janetta had shown them all to Jenny with these old glasses. But best of all was the lighthouse. It was on an island, all the way across the bay, at the entrance to Collingwood harbor. As Jenny adjusted the glasses, it sprang into view, tall, white and majestic, thrusting skyward. It looked different every day. On foggy days you couldn't see it at all, but today it was at its best.

"An omen!" Aunt Janetta used to declare. Nothing could go wrong on a day when the lighthouse was at its best!

Thoughtful now, Jenny replaced the glasses on the table and stood, staring out at the bay. "As many moods as a young girl," Aunt Janetta used to say and, indeed, just like the lighthouse, the bay looked different every day, sometimes every hour. Today, it was like a mirror, calm and welcoming.

I should be devastated, Jenny thought. My marriage has come to an end and, with it, my working life; everything I used to think was important. She had felt that wrenching grief in the parking lot of the plaza. It had seemed then that her life was in ruins, but now, she thought, surprised, now I am happy.

It was true. She could only stay for a few weeks, and Aunt Janetta wasn't here, but Jenny could feel a wondering, wonderful peace stealing over her.

She had come home.

III

> *"His insignia were thus the key which opens and closes the door, and the stick which porters employed to drive away those who had no right to cross the threshold."*
>
> – New Larousse Encyclopedia of Mythology

"Who the hell are you?"

Jenny nearly jumped out of her skin as a deep voice interrupted her reverie at the window. She whirled to face the intruder.

"Who the hell are *you*?" she asked in a shaky voice as she made out a tall, shadowy figure. He moved and suddenly the room was filled with light. Jenny was facing an old man, grizzled but erect, with startling blue eyes and an unruly, silver beard. She could see that the beard covered most, but not all, of the terrible scars that marred his face and her eyes dropped to his hands, also covered with scars.

"Wes Urquhart!" Jenny took a deep breath. "Gosh, you scared me!"

The old man smiled, his whole face lighting up. He glanced down sheepishly at the poker he held in his right hand.

"You scared me, too, Jenny Canal," he admitted. "As I guess you can see." He put the poker back down beside the huge stone fireplace that was another of the glories of Janus. "I thought someone had broken in."

Jenny looked curiously at the man. Wes Urquhart, she knew, lived next door to Aunt Janetta. The two of them had been friends. Over the years, Jenny had met him occasionally, shared a few meals with him when her aunt had taken pity on the bachelor next door and invited him for supper. That's why they had recognized each other, albeit a bit belatedly. Now, Jenny found herself wondering just how close her aunt and this man had been.

"I've been looking after the place for your aunt," he said in answer to her unspoken question.

"Oh, the garden!" Jenny exclaimed. "I wondered. It looks nice, Wes."

Wes shrugged.

"The garden was important to your aunt," he said abruptly. "I couldn't let it go to wrack and ruin."

"I know, and thank you. Although, you know, it's bound to go," Jenny added hesitantly.

The old man nodded glumly. It was something they both knew. Wasaga Beach was in a transition stage these days. All up and down the shore, people were buying up the old cottages, tearing them down and building big, new homes in their place. That was almost certain to happen to Janus. It was a beautiful old house made of solid wooden logs with spacious rooms, not to mention the glorious front window. And the fireplace. But it wasn't modern enough, no en suite bathrooms, no ceramic tile in the kitchen. So the house would go. And when they brought the bulldozers in, the garden would go, too.

"I will look after Janetta's garden until a sold sign goes up on the property," Wes said determinedly. "After that, it's nothing to do with me."

The old man looked at Jenny, his eyes softening.

"But I'm forgetting my manners," he exclaimed. "It's nice to see you, Jenny. Welcome! Here, let me light a fire for you."

To her surprise, Jenny saw that a fresh fire was already laid in the stone grate. A brush of a match from the mantel and flames sprung up instantly, casting a warm glow around the room. Jenny stared at the fire, remembering the hundreds of times she and her aunt had sat in front of it. Look into the flames, her aunt had urged her, ask it questions, dream your dreams. The fire has answers for you.

"Oh, it's all the same, hasn't changed a bit," Jenny breathed, looking around the room. Aunt Janetta had been a talented artist and one of the end walls had always been reserved for her latest paintings. The focus of the back wall was, of course, the fireplace. The other end wall was devoted to the illustrations for children's books that she had always made her living from. We all have to eat, she'd say, so the one deserves as much attention as the other.

With an effort, Jenny wrenched her attention back to Wes.

"You're up for the day? Overnight?" he was inquiring. "Your husband with you?"

Jenny squared her shoulders. It wasn't any of Wes' business, really, but she had to start acknowledging it somewhere.

"Bram and I are separating," she explained. "So I thought I'd stay here for a few weeks, until the house is sold."

The old man's eyes flashed. "Now you come!" he muttered.

Jenny stiffened. She knew exactly what he meant. When her aunt was dying in Collingwood Hospital, Jenny had wanted to be with her. But it had been impossible.

I should have been here, Jenny thought now, if only to celebrate how close we always were, all the years she helped me. Maybe I could have helped her. But Bram wouldn't hear of her coming to Wasaga Beach to stay, even for a few weeks. He had absolutely refused to consider it; she was needed at the gallery, he said, her place was with him. And so Jenny had done what she could, sending flowers every three days, books and magazines once a week, funny notes and sketches daily. She had made a few flying trips to the hospital on the sly, always rushed, always frantic that Bram would find out.

Why did I care? she thought now. I should have insisted. But obedience to Bram's wishes had been an old habit—it had taken the cataclysm of Shay to shake her loose from that. And Bram had always disliked Janetta intensely, probably because she would never allow her work to be sold in his gallery. The feeling had been mutual, Janetta had made no bones about her distaste for Jenny's husband.

"I did the best I could," she said now, helplessly, knowing it hadn't been good enough. But Wes was shaking his head.

"I'm sorry, Jenny, I had no right to say that," he said. "Janetta would be furious. She was always showing me the flowers and books you sent. She had your sketches pinned up on the wall next to the bed where she could see them. And she said that, too. 'Jenny's a good girl,' she'd say. 'She's doing the best she can.' "

Jenny felt tears sting her eyes. But Wes was continuing.

"It was mostly me," he was saying now. "I could have used some help those last few days. It was . . . well, it was pretty bad."

In the silence that followed, Jenny acutely felt all the

things he wasn't saying, how terrible it must have been to watch a once-vibrant woman fail, and slip away. She realized suddenly that this man and her aunt had been extremely close, closer than she'd ever realized.

"I'm glad you were there for her," she stammered. "I wish I'd been there, too."

Wes shrugged. "Your aunt meant a lot to me," he said simply. Then he brightened. "Course, I had William, though he didn't know Janetta very well, but he looked out for me."

"William?"

"My nephew," he said briefly. "Came to live with me last year."

Suddenly, Wes seemed to remember something.

"So, you're staying for awhile?" he said slowly. "It's funny, your aunt said she thought you might. Gave me a letter to give to you if you did." He reached into his pocket and withdrew a big, old-fashioned wallet. He opened it and took out a dog-eared envelope.

"I've been carrying it around with me since a week before she died," he said apologetically. "It's not in the best of shape."

Hesitantly, Jenny took the letter from him. What could it say?

"Thank you," she said. "I'll read it later, tonight, when I can concentrate."

And suddenly their conversation, which had taken on a strange intimacy, was over. Wes took his leave, insisting she call on him for anything she needed, "anything at all." Jenny saw him to the door, noting a battered old pickup truck in the driveway behind her car. A tall man, big and dark, was leaning on the fender. He straightened when he saw Wes, climbed into the truck and started it.

William, Jenny realized. And only then did she make sense of a fleeting impression she'd had earlier. There had actually been two figures in the dim and darkened living room. And when she'd turned and spoken Wes' name, the other one had faded into the hallway.

It had been William, she thought now, being tactful, but still looking out for his uncle. The thought made Jenny feel wistful.

And slightly ashamed. I wish I'd had the guts to do the same, she thought.

IV

"Janus was the god of all means of communication."
– New Larousse Encyclopedia of Mythology

Jenny stretched out in one of the soft, leather wingback chairs in front of the fireplace, a glass of wine next to her. It was Chianti, from one of the many bottles her aunt had laid down over the years. She had a pretty good wine cellar for an old lady!

After her encounter with Wes, Jenny had driven to the grocery store and stocked up on food. She'd also picked up some fresh underwear and socks. Right now she was snuggled into a soft, old, flannel shirt of her aunt's, a faded blue, that she had worn many times before. And jeans. She didn't regret leaving her clothes behind. They had all been gallery clothes—Bram clothes really—business suits, skirts, heels. He had never liked her in jeans. Old and comfortable weren't part of his vocabulary. "Remember your image," he'd say whenever she appeared in a sweatshirt or denim.

"Fuck my image," she thought violently. It had never been her's anyway, just Bram's. "And fuck Bram, too!"

Suddenly, she giggled. That was Shay's job now. Funny, she couldn't care less!

Jenny turned her attention to the letter from her aunt. It

had been on her mind all day. Now, slowly, she tore open the envelope. She had saved the letter till now, so she could concentrate on this last communication from her aunt. She smiled as she saw the familiar handwriting, jagged and avant garde in bold, black ink.

My dear Jenny, it said. *If you're reading this, it means you're staying at Janus. I'm so glad, my dear! I can almost see you in front of the fire, wearing that old, blue shirt of mine. You always did love Janus, almost as much as me. Enjoy it.*

God, how well Aunt Janetta knew her. Jenny kept reading.

I don't know your circumstances of course. If you're just here for a quick visit and everything is fine in your life, then that's one thing. But I have the idea you and Bram might be almost at the end of the road and, if that's the case, I hope you don't think of it as an ending. It is a beginning, Jenny, a door opening, and a new world lies before you, full of opportunity. Make the most of it, my dear – and no regrets!

How had she known? Jenny shook her head in amazement.

Since you're here, I want to ask if you'd look after the garden. I imagine Wes is doing it, but he shouldn't be. His arthritis is very painful just now and digging and planting and weeding won't help. So I want YOU to put in the summer bedding plants, help the old perennials along.

And I want to make a special request. For a long time now, I have been thinking about putting in a pond, just east of the garden path in that sandy patch behind the cottage next to the house. Kidney-shaped. With a fountain! And water lilies! It will be beautiful! Will you make this pond for me, Jenny? I have included detailed plans and instructions at the end of this letter. It's not as hard as you may think.

Please do this one last thing for your old aunt, Jenny. It will be a kind of memorial to the wonderful summers we spent together here when you were a girl. And even if the bulldozers rip it out in a few weeks, it will have been there for one brief, shining moment. Beauty is always transitory — and worth the more for it! It will make me happy.

Humor me in this, Jenny. Please. Think of it as a labor of love. Do it yourself, everything, even the digging. Don't let Wes or that nephew of his help. This will be your last gift to me, my dear, and I thank you for it. You always were a good girl, and I love you very much. Good luck! Aunt Janetta.

"Jesus Christ!" Jenny cast the letter aside and jumped up. Clearly Aunt Janetta had lost her mind! She began to pace in front of the fireplace. How the hell was she supposed to look after the garden? When she had recognized the tulips and daffodils earlier today, that had been the extent of her gardening knowledge. Bedding plants? What the hell were they?

And a pond? Build a pond? DIG a pond? But that was crazy! She wouldn't know where to start! No way!

Well, she wouldn't do it, that's all. It was too bad, but Aunt Janetta would just have to do without her pond. She wouldn't know. And what was the point of building it when it would all be torn up in a few weeks anyway? No way! No way! No way!

Jenny stopped as a memory came to her out of the blue. Aunt Janetta used to grow these spectacular flowers. Huge! What were they called? Allium. That was it! From the onion family, Aunt Janetta had told her. They were gorgeous. But when the big heads, made up of thousands of tiny purple florets died, they looked pretty ugly, their brown heads looming mournfully over the garden. So, Aunt Janetta spray-painted them. An electric blue. And they had fooled everyone. One time, a particularly irritating old man, a guest at one of the cottages, had been wandering around the garden, commenting on the weeds, the poor soil, what he called the general disorder of Aunt Janetta's admittedly slightly wild garden. But he had fallen in love with the painted allium. He couldn't stop exclaiming over them. And he never dreamed they'd been painted. Jenny and Aunt Janetta had laughed till they cried over that.

"Hell!" Jenny flung herself back into the chair. Damn it anyway! She didn't have one clue about it. But, yes! Okay! She would build the goddamn pond! Of course. How could she not? Jenny had spent every summer of her life here until she married Bram. Just she and her aunt. Jenny sighed and began to study the plans.

Aunt Janetta would have her pond.

V

"Janus was also the god of beginnings."
– New Larousse Encyclopedia of Mythology

It wasn't, after all, that complicated. Just hard work.

Lots of hard work!

Jenny had spent the past two days hauling rocks. She had gone to the garden centre out on the highway and had purchased a vinyl liner for the pond. And rocks. Many, many rocks.

One thousand, three hundred and twenty pounds of rocks to be exact. She knew this because they sold them by weight. It had taken five trips in her old Datsun to bring all the rocks home. And then they had to be moved up the garden path. Fortunately, she'd found an old dolly in the garage that had made it easier. Not easy, just easier. Even now, Jenny could hardly believe she'd moved one thousand, three hundred and twenty pounds of rocks.

Mentally, Jenny reviewed the plan. Trace a kidney shape in the sand. Dig it out to a depth of about two feet. Place the liner in it so the edges overlapped the edges of the pond. Place the flat rocks she'd bought over the liner. Then put the pretty rocks, the ones with the indentations and odd holes and moss, on top of the flat rocks. Add water. And that was that! The fountain could come later.

"I can do this," Jenny muttered as she started to dig.

An hour later, she wasn't so sure. Christ, it was just sand. It shouldn't be so hard to dig. But years behind the counter in an art gallery hadn't exactly suited her for manual labor. This was hard work! But still, she was getting there. The pond was about half dug.

Suddenly, Jenny's shovel hit metal, deep in the sand. What fresh hell was this? Some bloody old tin can, she thought, jabbing at it viciously. There had been a few of them already.

But no, this was different. Bigger. Wider. More cautiously, Jenny began to shift the sand above it. A few minutes later, she dropped the shovel and stared.

She was looking at an old metal box. On top of it, in bright red letters, was painted the word "Jenny." She tried to lift it, but it wouldn't budge. It took another ten minutes with the shovel before she could lift it free, heave it up to the side of the hole.

The top opened easily on freshly oiled hinges. Freshly oiled? What the hell? Inside was an old book, a journal by the look of it, bound in soft leather. And an envelope—with her name on it. What the hell was this? A goddamn treasure hunt? Irritated, Jenny tore open the letter. Yes, it was in her aunt's handwriting.

Dear Jenny, it began. *Don't be annoyed. Think of all this as a treasure hunt – with witty clues supplied by your brilliant aunt.*

Jenny felt her irritation fade. Half unwillingly, she laughed. Aunt Janetta always had been one step ahead of her. And yeah, in a way it was kind of fun, getting these letters from her when she was dead and gone. Quite wonderful, really. Like an unexpected gift.

Darling girl, if you're reading this letter, it means you've found the box. And that means you're building my pond! Thank you, thank you, thank you! It will be beautiful, I know.

I hid the box in the sand — well, Wes did — because I wanted you to have this journal. You know I spent some time in Venice when I was just 21. And you know I have always, always loved Venice. A very special city, my dear, and the one our family came from several generations ago. I used to talk to you about Venice, I remember, but I never told you the whole story. You were just a girl and it wouldn't have done to shake your faith in your aunt's morals, would it? It's different now. Now I think you MUST be without Bram — he would never let you waste time building a pond! And I want to give you some sense of the opportunities out there — if only you go looking for them! I don't mean you should pack up and go to Venice — though it wouldn't be a bad idea — but I just want you to stay open. Live your life, don't just endure it! The time I spent in Venice was the most wonderful of my life — though there were some good times later, too. You were a big part of what made them good, my dear. But as I said, Venice was special. And now I want to share it with you.

Forgive all the mystery, dear girl. I could have just handed you the journal, but I suppose I felt that as long as you were with Bram, operating that sterile little gallery of his, you wouldn't understand. Now I think you will. And I also suppose that I wanted to know you were committed — to me, to Janus, to freedom, whatever — before I entrusted this journal to you. I want you to be engaged!!!!!!!

Now for heaven's sake, do carry on with the pond! You are an absolute doll to build it for me! I can't wait to see how it turns out. And yes, my dear, never doubt that I will know.

Somehow. I'm sure of it. So, save the journal for a night in front of the fire – AND GET BACK TO WORK! Right now! Love, Aunt Janetta.

Jenny slowly raised her head from the letter, aware that she was laughing and crying, all at the same time. What a woman Aunt Janetta had been! How had she known it would soon be over for Bram and her? Sterile little gallery indeed. How furious Bram would be if he heard that. But she was right. The gallery wasn't little, of course, Bram had prided himself on owning one of the biggest galleries in the Greater Toronto Area. But it was sterile. Bram had never been interested in art, only in what would sell. Jenny had sometimes thought he might as well have been selling vacuum cleaners for all the interest he took in the product – a thought she had hastily buried as disloyal. But it was true, she thought now. He had loaded up the gallery with wildlife prints and cutesy paintings of English cottages with thatched roofs. He hadn't quite sunk to Elvis on velvet, but he might have if he'd thought it would sell. And he'd always quashed Jenny's occasional efforts to introduce something more interesting, encourage some younger artists. "I'm not running a charity for OCA students," he'd sneer, referring to the Ontario College of Art. And eventually Jenny had given up without even realizing it. It had been a long time since she'd tried to do anything at the gallery except take the money and balance the books.

Jenny looked at the journal. Suddenly, she couldn't wait to start reading it. She had always been curious about her aunt's time in Venice, had always had the sense that there was more to the story. And now the story was right here, waiting for her.

But, no. Her aunt was right. Better stick to the pond for

now. She would read the journal tonight—something to look forward to! Jenny carried the metal box over to the house and placed it inside the back door. Then, with a groan, she returned to the pond. Bloody thing! *And I thought the slaves had been freed,* she thought!

Several hours later, she was almost done. The rest of the digging had been uneventful. Placing the vinyl liner had been no problem either, despite the fact that Jenny had to get right in the hole to stomp it into the corners where the walls had started their upward climb. The rocks, though, had been a major damn chore. God, they were heavy. But Jenny had become interested in the process despite herself and had spent some extra time placing the rocks where they looked the nicest. They were lovely rocks—if a rock could be lovely—and Jenny had found herself wanting to display them so that the most interesting formations, the lunar landscapes of holes and mossy hillocks, the craggy bits, showed. She had also thrown rocks into the bottom of the pond to cover the liner. Now Jenny dragged the hose over to the pond and turned it on. It would take a while to fill. Jenny found that, again despite herself, she couldn't wait to see what it looked like filled with water.

Just then Jenny saw a short, pudgy man bustling up the walk. He was wearing a tie. A tie at Wasaga Beach?

"Hello," the man said, thrusting his hand out. "You must be Jenny Canal. I'm Wally Thornton, your real estate agent . . . what are you doing!?" he said in tones of horror as he caught site of the construction zone.

"And here I thought it was beginning to look like a pond," Jenny said dryly. "That's what I'm doing. Building a pond."

"But that's ridiculous!" he exclaimed. "This place will be

sold soon and all this rubbish will be cleared out."

Jenny's eyes narrowed.

"Rubbish?" she inquired.

He caught the suddenly dangerous tone of her voice and changed tack.

"Well, maybe not rubbish. But it's not exactly to modern taste, is it? All these flowers and vines and statues with no clothes on," he said, looking at Aphrodite with distaste. "Your aunt was a very eccentric lady, I fear. The new people will probably just want some foundation shrubs and a nice lawn. And, of course, that rundown old house and all these cottages will have to go."

"Eccentric! Rundown!" Jenny's voice was incredulous. "My aunt kept her house in excellent shape. And this is a beautiful garden! Are you nuts?"

Wally Thornton looked shocked.

"Now, now, there's no need to get testy," he said. "I just mean that the new people will build something more suitable, perhaps a house with easy-care aluminum siding. And, of course, most of these trees and bushes will have to go. It's a quite a tangle in here, isn't it?"

Jenny stared at the man. The pines? The cedars? They were going to chop them down? Her aunt's beloved mock cherry, gone? And her wonderful bushes, the flowering almond, the spirea, the japonica, the forsythia? All gone? Wally Thornton wasn't telling her anything she hadn't known, though he was certainly more obnoxious about it than most. But, dear God, a nice lawn? Easy-care aluminum siding?

Suddenly Jenny felt as if she'd been in a boat, a boat pitching and tossing on stormy waters. Rain and fog all around. And now the fog had lifted and she found herself in an estuary, a place of calm waters and sunny skies. A place to stay.

She didn't know what she was going to say until she said it.

"I'm sorry, Mr. Thornton, but I've changed my mind," she heard herself say. "Janus is not for sale."

Wally Thornton reacted angrily.

"You can't change your mind," he exclaimed.

"Yes, I can."

"You signed a contract with me!" he persisted.

Jenny saw red.

"Well, I just unsigned it," she snapped. She marched up the path to the street, Thornton right behind her, protesting. Jenny grabbed the For Sale and yanked it out of the ground, throwing it at Thornton's feet.

"I said Janus is not for sale!" she said, matching his anger with her own.

"And I said you can't do that!" Thornton shouted.

"Oh yes I can!"

"No, you can't!"

Impasse! The two were glaring at each other, seething with fury, when a third voice intervened.

"A little tension here," Wes Urquhart observed mildly. He had been putting the garbage out next door when he heard the shouting. "What seems to be the problem?"

It didn't take long for Wes to get the gist of the argument, even with both of them talking at once. He pursed his lips in a soundless whistle and turned to Jenny.

"Jenny, are you sure you want to do this?" he asked. "Really sure? You're not just mad at Wally here?"

Jenny took a deep breath. "I've never been more sure of anything in my life," she declared.

Wes turned to Thornton.

"You heard the lady, Wally, she doesn't want to sell." He held up a hand as Thornton began to sputter furiously.

"I know she signed a listing with you. But these things aren't carved in stone. You can tear it up." Wes ignored Thornton's anger, continuing to speak calmly.

"As you know, I build lots of houses around the beach." Jenny had vaguely known that Wes owned a construction company. GG construction it was called. She had never understood the name. "And I could swing some of the listings your way, make up for the commission you're losing here," Wes continued.

Thornton stopped in mid-rant.

"I thought your nephew was running the company now," he said suspiciously.

"He is," Wes replied. "And doing a great job of it, too. But I think you'll find he still listens to his uncle—if it's something I think is important."

For the first time, Wes' voice took on the hint of a threat.

"And I do think this is important, Wally."

Thornton took the hint.

"What about that street your nephew is building?" he asked, suddenly interested. "I hear it's quite something. Could I have the listings on it?"

Wes shook his head.

"That's William's baby, I won't interfere with that," he said. "But we're just finishing two houses at the south end of town and a real nice one on the river, another waterfront for you. I could pretty much guarantee you the listings on them."

Thornton wasn't about to give up without a fight.

"I've spent money advertising this property," he blustered.

"I'm sure you have," Wes answered smoothly. "And I'm sure Jenny will reimburse you—just send her the receipts," he added sternly. He didn't want any padded bills.

Thornton nodded slowly. It was obvious he didn't want to make an enemy out of Wes Urquhart.

"All right then," he said. "I'll tear up the listing." He picked up the sign and threw it in the back seat of his car.

"You're lucky you have friends," he said snidely to Jenny. It was his parting thrust. In silence, they watched him drive away. Jenny turned to Wes.

"I am lucky I have friends," she said soberly. "Thank you very much, Wes."

A slow grin came over the old face.

"You got a temper just like your aunt's," he said. "I could have sworn it was Janetta standing here screaming at that jackass."

Screaming? Jenny felt herself flush.

"You really saved me, Wes. I appreciate it."

Wes shrugged. "Glad to help." He looked at her more closely. "You're filthy, girl!" he exclaimed. "What have you been doing?"

Jenny laughed.

"I know I am," she said. "I've been building a bloody pond, that's what I've been doing."

A look of wonder spread over Wes' face.

"So it's all worked out just like she thought," he said. "You're keeping Janus and you're actually building the pond. Uh, you find anything when you were digging in there?"

Now it was Jenny's turn to grin.

"Yes, I found the damn box," she said. "I take it you're

the one who buried it."

"Janetta wanted me to," he said simply. "But, listen, if you're actually building the pond, then William and I have some things for you. We'll be right over!"

And, just like that, Wes hurried away.

Puzzled, Jenny watched him turn into his own driveway. It sure was nice of him to help me out, though, she thought. With a signed contract, things might have gotten sticky.

Suddenly, Jenny remembered the hose. Yikes! She hurried up through the garden. My garden now, she thought happily. My beach, my house, my mock cherry tree! She patted Aphrodite fondly on the bum as she passed.

"Okay, Aunt Janetta," she murmured. "I am now engaged!"

VI

"Janus had an essential role in the creation of the world."
– New Larousse Encyclopedia of Mythology

The pond was not quite overflowing when Jenny got back to it. Thankfully, she shut the hose off. It really does look pretty, she thought, even if it's still kind of raw. She'd have to haul away the piles of sand, back to the beach. And go shopping for a fountain. But the rocks looked great! And the sun was glinting off the water in the pond, promising even more beauty when she got everything arranged. Jenny was just winding up the hose when Wes and William came up the garden path — Wes carrying a tall, ungainly parcel wrapped in brown paper; William carrying a smaller parcel and a shopping bag.

"Jenny, this is William," Wes said.

The two nodded at each other.

"So, what do you think?" Jenny said, gesturing to the pond. "Turned out pretty good, didn't it?"

"Wow, I'll say!" William was regarding the pond with surprise. "It's wonderful! You dug this out, moved all these rocks by yourself?"

"For my sins," Jenny laughed. "To be honest, I didn't think I could do it. But I managed," she said with satisfaction.

"You should have told me!" William exclaimed. "I'd have been glad to help."

Solemnly, Jenny shook her head.

"Nope. Aunt Janetta wanted me to do it all myself—just in case I found some buried treasure," she said, winking at Wes. He laughed.

"Janetta might have wanted you to do it yourself, but I don't think she'd say no to a couple of gifts," he said.

"Ohhhh, I love gifts," Jenny joked.

"Now, this one is special." Wes looked suddenly sheepish. "At least I think it is."

As Wes tore the brown paper off, Jenny caught her breath. Special? I'll say, she thought, unconsciously echoing William. What emerged was a fountain, about six feet tall, made of wood, all handcarved. It consisted of three tall lilies and, further down the stems, a number of broad leaves. It was polished to a golden gleam and the carving was stunning, even down to the veins on the leaves.

It was the most beautiful thing Jenny had ever seen.

Wes was busy explaining.

"See, the stems are hollow so the water comes up the stems and out the flowers. It falls onto the leaves and from there, in a wider arc, it falls back into the pond. Should be quite graceful. And look here, the leaves are slightly cupped so they'll hold some water, too. I think you'll find the birds use them as birdbaths, which should be pretty." He paused. "It's not usual to use wood as a fountain. But I fibreglassed it pretty good, so it shouldn't rot."

"You!" Jenny stared at Wes in astonishment. "You made this?"

William frowned.

"Of course he did!" William exclaimed. "Uncle Wes is a brilliant carver. Famous, too. He did that head of Janus out front that your aunt liked so much and he has carvings in galleries all across Canada."

This was Aunt Janetta's helpful neighbor in a whole new light! But it made sense, she thought. Aunt Janetta, being an artist, would have appreciated this kind of skill. No wonder they were such good friends.

"I'm sorry," she said slowly. "I didn't know. I always liked that head, too. I just never knew who'd carved it. But this, Wes, this is . . . ." At a loss for words, Jenny fell back on her first thought. "It's the most beautiful thing I've ever seen!"

Wes looked pleased. Embarrassed, but pleased.

"Glad you like it," he said gruffly. "Now, I've got a pump here. Let's see if it works. William, run that cord over to an outlet, would you?"

William found an outlet at the side of the house and laid the extension cord beside it. Then he ran the cord across the garden path to the pond. "We can dig that in later," he said. The cord was attached to the pump and the pump to the fountain. Then carefully, the two men lowered the fountain into the water. William walked back to the cord.

"Ready?" he called. Then he plugged the cord into the outlet.

For a moment, nothing happened. Then there was a gurgle, another gurgle, and suddenly water shot out of the three flower heads, onto the leaves and, from there, back into the pond. It was graceful, just like Wes had prophesied. In fact, it was absolutely wonderful. Jenny felt a manic joy sweep over her.

Like a young girl, she began running from one spot in

the garden to another.

"It's beautiful from here," she called. "And it's lovely from here, too. Oh look, it's gorgeous from here." Suddenly she darted behind Aphrodite. The two men heard another squeal of pleasure. "Ohhhhh, you can hear it even when you can't see it! Is there anything nicer than the sound of running water?"

Literally capering with joy, Jenny ran back to the pond and threw her arms around Wes. He looked startled, then laughed and hugged her back. William was grinning broadly. Jenny kissed Wes on the cheek.

"Wes, it's a work of art," she said. "It is the most beautiful fountain in the whole world, I'm sure of that! I love it! Thank you very, very much!"

Now it was Jenny's turn to look embarrassed.

"God, you must think I'm an idiot," she said, calming down at last. "But this means so much to me. Wes, I'll treasure it. Forever."

Wes swallowed hard. This girl was so much like Janetta! Her enthusiasm, her joy, even her fury earlier this afternoon, all wrapped up in one very attractive package! A thought occurred to him. William should get on the ball there. Hmmmm, an interesting idea. None of my business, of course, he thought. Still, a little nudge wouldn't hurt.

On second thought, maybe a nudge wasn't necessary. William was walking toward Jenny now, his eyes drinking in every inch of her. In his hands was the package he'd carried over.

"Now, that's a tough act to follow," he chuckled. "But Uncle Wes' fountain was the main event anyway. This is just a little adjunct."

"I love adjuncts," Jenny joked, echoing her earlier comment.

William laughed and tore off the wrapping. It was another fountain, but this one was very different. It was a kind of abstract metal piece made up of copper pipes of all sizes, all bundled together with brass bands. It was considerably shorter than the wooden lilies and completely different, but it had a presence all its own.

"It's very handsome," Jenny exclaimed. "Where did you get it?"

William laughed. "I may be an architect, not an artist..."

Jenny interrupted him.

"An architect?" she said, surprised. "I thought you were a builder."

"I'm both," he said. "There's no point having these great ideas if you can't make them work in real life."

Another fresh look at another neighbor. What an interesting day, Jenny thought. But William was continuing.

"As I was saying, I'm not an artist, but I may have a creative bone or two in my body. I decided it shouldn't be beyond me to come up with something interesting — and here it is!"

"It is interesting," Wes spoke up. "Nice composition, and the brass bands with the copper pipes work very well. We may make an artist out of you yet, my boy."

"You'll have your work cut out for you," William laughed. "No, Jenny, the real feature of your pond is definitely Uncle Wes' fountain. But this is for the other end. It won't detract from the flower fountain because its spray is entirely different, lower, more diffused. It will look kind of like a shallow, upside-down bowl made of water, that's all. But the important thing is it will aerate both ends of the pond. You'll need that."

"I will?" Jenny said blankly. "Why?"

William looked surprised. "For the fish, of course!"

"The fish?" Jenny all but shrieked. "I don't have any fish!"

Now both men were laughing.

"Yes, you do," William grinned. He opened the bag he'd brought with him and pulled out a plastic bag filled with water—and fish.

Now Jenny did shriek.

"I can't have any fish," Jenny gasped. "I don't know how to look after them!"

"It's easy." William groped in his pocket, drew out a phial of fish food. "Just give them some of this every day."

"No fish!" Jenny sounded definite.

William raised an eyebrow. "What do you think Uncle Wes?" he asked.

"Janetta would have wanted fish," Wes said firmly.

Jenny knew when she'd been beaten. Resignedly, she watched as William tipped them into the pond. "I got them acclimatized to tap water over at the house," he explained. "Otherwise we'd have to leave the bag in the pond for a couple of hours." There were about ten of them, all very tiny, and once in the water, they instantly disappeared among the rocks at the bottom of the pond. William looked disappointed.

"The idea was that Jenny would enjoy watching them swim around," he said accusingly to his uncle. "But you can't even see them! I thought you said this would work!"

Wes shrugged.

"They're tiny now, but fish grow to their environment. Just wait, in a few weeks they'll be visible."

Suddenly the two men became very male. They hooked

up the second fountain. It looked very nice. They dug the lines in, lifting one of the concrete slabs in the garden path without much effort. They gave her instructions, many instructions, about how to clean the fountains, how to feed the fish, how to check the water quality. Jenny's head began to spin. Good thing they just live next door, she thought wryly. When they quit fussing, she had an idea.

"You guys want to stay for supper?" she asked. "I have some spaghetti sauce on the stove."

Wes' eyes lit up.

"It taste anything like Janetta's?" he asked hopefully.

Jenny laughed. "Well, she taught me how to make it. It should."

Wes looked happy. "You got yourself a couple of guests," he declared, throwing an arm around William, tugging him toward the house. "I imagine there's some Chianti, too," he told him confidentially. "Janetta always kept good Chianti."

Jenny looked at the pond. She'd done it! Just the way her aunt wanted. And the fountains looked spectacular. What marvelous gifts! And what marvelous guys—she was lucky to have them as friends. For a moment, Jenny closed her eyes, listening to the burble of the falling water. Perfect! Then she followed the men.

"Of course there's good Chianti," she called out.

VII

January 15, 1939

I can hardly believe it, but here I am, at last, in Venice! Venezia! Bella Venezia!

Venice really is the most wonderful city, a city of bells and bridges, of ancient buildings and tiny squares, narrow passageways and window boxes spilling with flowers. And water! I knew about the canals, of course — who does not? — but I hadn't realized how central they were to the very fact of Venice. They do everything by boat here — even collect the garbage! The local buses are boats called vaporettos. And the gondolas! They are like stately black swans gliding proudly upon the waters.

I have found a room in a pensione. It is tiny and on the fourth floor — I shall lose weight, running up and down the stairs! But, although small, it has everything I need, a comfortable double bed, a wardrobe for my clothes, a tiny icebox and a hotplate. I won't be roasting any turkeys here, but it will do for soup and spaghetti and omelettes. My needs are simple — and I am determined to keep them that way. Best of all are two tall windows, a desk in front of one. I shall set up my easel at the other. The view is of chimneys and pitched roofs, all clothed in that wonderful Italian tile in a dozen shades of terra cotta. Just below is a canal, not the Grand Canal, of course, just a small, rather domestic canal with washing strung over it and boats of every description tied to tall poles set into the water at odd angles.

I found this pensione through the art school and, indeed, we are all art students here. These are the people I shall share my life with for the next twelve months. I can tell already that my best friend will be probably be Dorothea, an English girl in the very next room. She is blonde and beautiful and very lively. Great fun!

I was quite intimidated when I met the students for first time. They are all so sophisticated and intellectual. I hope they do not paint better than me. But they were all very friendly. Perhaps I, too, seemed sophisticated. I hope so, I even wore my new black stockings. Daddy disliked them very much when he saw them, I recall, but I told him that all art students wear black stockings — well, the women at least! He just laughed and waved his hands in the air. "Do what you like, my little bird," he said. "This is your time to fly." I hope it is. Mama didn't want me to come at all, but Daddy said it would be okay. "She has a head on her shoulders, our Janetta," he told my mother. "It will be good for her to see the city of our ancestors, especially the great Antonio Canaletto."

In fact, our connection with the artist Canaletto is tenuous, more of a family legend than bare fact. The details are lost in time. But my father believes it and so do I. We have the same name, Canal, even if he was known as Canaletto because his father was living at the same time and was also an artist — well, actually, a set painter for the theatre. But in the same realm. Canaletto meant "the younger Canal," perhaps literally the small Canal. Names seemed more fluid then. Antonio Canaletto was also known, at different periods in his life, as Canale, Canaleto, Canaletti! He even signed his name differently on various documents. How pleasant to wake up each morning and sign your name, depending on how the whim takes you! I have always been just plain Janetta Canal.

Besides Dorothea, there is a German girl named Ruth, very tall and athletic. She intends to get a small rowboat and row all over Venice. I wonder if she will. And there is Teresa, a Portugese girl, very slight and short and dark.

Among the men, there are John and George from New York. They seem rather aggressive, always giving their opinions as if they are unshakeable pronouncements. But friendly and down to earth. And there is Pierre from France, very slim and romantic, and Paulo from Spain. I do not think I will like him much. He is very dark and brooding. He has his eye on Teresa, but he frightens her, I think.

And, of course, there is "Byron." He arrived a week ago and, within a day, was given that nickname because of his good looks. He really is very handsome!

There are other students in the pensione, a pompous fellow from Germany, a very rough Pole, several more from France. But Dorothea, Ruth, Teresa, John, George, Pierre, Paulo, Byron and I will be taking classes together. They will be my closest friends.

"We few, we happy few, we band of brothers."

And sisters.

VIII

January 26, 1939

It has been more than a week since I have written. Well, I could not write, I was too busy living! But in the future I must try to do both. I don't want to end up back in Toronto with no record of my year in Venice. I will have my memories, of course, burnt bright into my mind. But a record would be useful, too. So I must be more diligent with this journal.

How I love this journal! The paper is handmade in Florence. It is very textured and creamy. And the covers are soft calfskin. Long leather strings wrap around it several times to hold it closed. It is a journal worthy to record the greatest adventure of my life.

Classes begin at the Academia tomorrow. This week has been devoted to getting to know Venice – at least a little. One day the whole group of us went to the Piazza de San Marco, the most famous square in the world. The first thing that struck me were the pigeons, literally thousands of them. They move in fluttering clouds from one visitor to the next, hoping for hand-outs. You can buy little bags of seeds to feed them. But it is a dangerous proceeding! They land on your arm, your shoulders, even your head. The internecine war is very fierce. Peck, peck, peck! They are very bold.

At the very end of the square is the Cathedral. What an amazing sight! Gilt on paint on carving on stone. It is very baroque, very rococco, like a huge, fancy wedding cake, with energetic bronze horses on top, instead of a plastic bride and groom. To be honest, it is a bit overdecorated for my North American tastes, but it is still an astonishing work of art. How odd to think of a building as a work of art, but here in Venice that is exactly what they are. Especially the churches. And especially the biggest church of all, the Cathedral. Toronto seems very far away.

I wanted to go through the Cathedral, but my friends had a different purpose in mind. They intended to visit Florian's. I am embarrassed to admit I had never heard of it, but now I know it is a very famous cafe and very old – it was opened in the 1700s, more than 200 years ago! And over the years, it has had many distinguished visitors, all the great artists and writers and musicians of the time. Byron and Keats and Shelley, Goethe, Wagner. I found it very moving to drink cappuccino in such company, my mind peopled the tiny tables and gilt chairs with all of them. The most famous place to meet at Florians is "under the Chinaman," a well-known painting, and so we gathered there. Florian's is a labyrinth of small rooms filled with fabulous paintings and fascinating people, men in dramatic, silk – lined cloaks, women in outrageous hats. A dozen languages swirl into the air, mixing with the smoke from cigars and cigarettes. The cafe offers unforgettable cakes and pastries, wonderful hot chocolate. But I like the cappuccino best. The whole square is lined with cafes and in nice weather there are tables outside and live music from small ensembles. I can't wait to see that!

We also visited the Rialto, the famous bridge. I remember the Shakespearean character Shylock from The Merchant of Venice calling out "What news on the Rialto?" I never understood that, what news could there be on a bridge? But now I do. For the Rialto is not like a bridge at all; it is more like a colorful street lined with shops, stuffed with exotic merchandise, the vendors standing out front hawking their wares. Only at the very top of the arched bridge are there openings where you can actually see you are on a bridge. We hung over the rail, marveling at the scene on the Grand Canal. Boats and gondolas moving in every direction, famous old palazzos on the banks of the canals, each sporting their coat of arms and their proud striped poles for the gondolas to tie up at. What a sight!

I want to speak of two things before I close to get ready for class in the morning. I am nervous, but excited about that.

First, Byron. I have come to see him in a different light. He is wonderfully handsome with a gay, romantic air about him, his black hair tumbling into his eyes, his body strong and well-muscled. He has a stunning profile, quite haunting in its classic beauty. I want to paint him! But his beauty goes beyond his looks. I am beginning to think he is quite the nicest man I have ever met. And I think he likes me!!!!! He held my hand on the Rialto, just for a moment, and he has asked me to go with him to a local trattoria for supper tomorrow night after our first day of classes. Just the two of us. It is only to discuss our impressions of the school, of course, but, well, I confess I am looking forward to it. We shall see.

The other thing is more serious. Indeed, I hardly know how to put it into words. The heady atmosphere of Venice has had the odd effect of sobering me, freshening my resolve. To be surrounded by the works of Titian and Tiepolo, to hear Vivaldi everywhere I go, to know my own ancestor, Antonio Canaletto, *painted these canals bursting with life and movement. All these great and talented men lived and worked in Venice — and I feel I must honor them by emulating them. My art will never be as good, but I will work, really work, at my art to make it the best I can. To honor their own.*

That is all I wanted to say.

IX

"Janus was the promoter of all initiative."
– New Larousse Encyclopedia of Mythology

What a glorious day! Jenny was wandering around the garden, morning coffee in hand. She paused by the pond. It had been several weeks since she had built it and everything was in order now—sand from the hole hauled away; she had even added water lilies. Six of them in their muddy baskets at the bottom of the pond. Almost instantly, they had begun to send up tendrils and leaves and buds and now, today—surely!—there would be a flower.

Yes! There it was, a delicate pink, stunning in its perfection. Jenny had read that water lilies were related to the lotus, the flower that the Buddhists held sacred. They saw the lotus as symbolic of the enlightened soul—beauty emerging from the muck and dross of everyday life. And its beauty was only enhanced by the sound of trickling water—the fountains were still going strong! Jenny sighed with pleasure. Aunt Janetta would have loved this pond.

Jenny continued her ramble through the garden. The blossoms on the mock cherry had come and gone. Just as Aunt Janetta had said, they were breathtaking in their beauty for one day and, the very next day, were gone, the pink petals carpeting the walks. Jenny had left them there until they turned brown. Even on the ground, they had turned the garden into an enchanted land of pink and rose.

Much to her surprise, Jenny had found she liked working in the garden. It was so peaceful, so soothing. And when you got into the slow rhythm of it, there were wonderful little surprises along the way. Jenny had nearly burst with excitement the day she saw her first hummingbird, jade green with a ruby-red throat, hovering over a flower. And she had been delighted when a family of robins took up residence in the old birdhouse, busily building a nest inside. She couldn't wait to see the fledglings.

Jenny had found, too, that she knew more about gardening than she realized. But perhaps that wasn't surprising — something certainly should have sunk in after all those years by Aunt Janetta's side. And whatever she didn't know, Aunt Janetta's huge shelf of gardening books could tell her. And so she had put in the bedding plants, sticking mostly to shade flowers. Sun for the flowers or shade from the old trees — that had always been Aunt Janetta's dilemma. She usually resolved it by just trimming the trees and planting lots of shade flowers. So Jenny had done the same thing, planting luscious tuberous begonias, pretty pink impatience, wildly colored coleus. She had even dared greatly and added a few innovations of her own. For one thing, she had planted pink geraniums in an astonishing array of clay pots and arranged them on an old table. She had also remembered her aunt bemoaning the fact that her sweet little morning glories struggled in the sandy soil, not blooming until September when, almost immediately, they were nipped and killed by the frost. Jenny had decided it shouldn't be impossible to get around that, so she had planted the morning glories in pots instead of in the ground, using extremely good soil and lots of fertilizer. And it had paid off. Already they were twining around the arbor and it wouldn't be long before they were in bloom—several months ahead of schedule!

Perhaps the biggest innovation Jenny had introduced was a flower bed running all around the pond, with only an open space on one side to feed the fish. To herself—but not to William—Jenny admitted to a sneaking affection for the fish. Wes had been right; they had grown enormously in just a few weeks and were now visible almost all the time, swimming in lazy circles. Jenny had taken to knocking hard on a rock before sprinkling their food into the pond, signaling dinner. It was great fun to watch them come boiling to the surface when she knocked. Jenny had taken some trouble with the flower bed around the pond, mixing and matching plants, so the bed was a brilliant, but perfectly balanced, sea of color.

She had even, hesitantly, painted a few pictures. Outdoor ones, on big boards. Brilliant sunflowers now hung by the pond. They looked pretty good, too! It had been years since Jenny had painted, but once, before Bram, it had been her whole life. She had even had a year of art college. I was going to be an artist, she thought now, a bit wistfully. Devote my life to art. And she was glad that, however tentatively, she had started painting again. She had forgotten the pure pleasure of spreading color, creating form.

Her inspection of the garden over, Jenny headed for the front, passing the allium as she went. They were in bloom now, but starting to die off. Almost time to bring out the spray paint. Jenny laughed. That was one tradition she would definitely keep up. It was just so much fun.

As Jenny emerged into the front courtyard of Janus, the

landscape changed entirely. Aunt Janetta had always kept the front in its natural state, just sand and cedars, beach and water, adding only a few pots of red geraniums for color. It made sense, too; you couldn't improve on this vista!

Jenny made her way to the bench at the very top of the beach. It was her favorite place to sit, in the early morning with a coffee, and at sunset with a glass of wine. And what sunsets! It was like having a ringside seat at a great spectacle as the sun set over the bay, turning the sky red and pink and orange, even violet.

The view was so pretty here, the bay running a few whitecaps in the freshening breeze, the sun glinting off the water. Even the lighthouse was visible to the naked eye. Reluctantly, Jenny turned her mind to a problem that had been nagging at her for days. Money. What the hell was she going to do about money? She had the $20,000 from her raid on Bram's safe, of course, but it was melting away. Rapidly. There was no mortgage on Janus, thank heavens. Aunt Janetta had paid it off years ago, but there was still heat and hydro, telephone. Jenny had just paid a big tax bill and reimbursed that idiot Thornton for his advertising and, well, the money was disappearing in a big hurry. Even the pond — the rocks hadn't been cheap, and the water lilies had a price beyond belief. Jenny had blithely ordered six, never thinking to ask how much they were. She had been horrified to discover they were $30 each. Good grief! One hundred and eighty dollars for six lousy water lilies!!! Jenny didn't begrudge the money, especially now that she'd seen how beautiful they were. But the point was that now she was keeping Janus, there would be no big payoff to smooth her immediate future. She needed an income.

I suppose I'll have to get a job, she thought unenthusiastically. Jenny had never been afraid of hard work, but she found herself surprisingly unwilling to leave Janus five or six days a week to earn a living. She wanted to stay right where she was, working in the garden, walking on the beach.

Well, you can't, she told herself. There was no sense waiting until her money was gone and then flying into a panic. The time to deal with the problem was now, while she still had a cushion. Under no circumstances was she going to ask Bram for money. I'll starve first, she vowed.

Jenny glanced around the courtyard. Four of her aunt's cottages were built in a u-shape around the front courtyard. Two others, less desireable without a water view, were back under the trees. Aunt Janetta had the right idea, she thought idly, she just rented out the cottages and that gave her enough . . .

Christ! Jenny sat bolt upright as the idea came to her. A moment later she sagged as good sense intervened. There was no way she could rent the cottages out. They had been shut up for ten years, they were probably over-run with mice and spiders and heaven know what else! She shuddered to think of what they must be like: ratty old furniture, cranky, outdated appliances. Musty. Damp. No, forget it. Bad idea.

But she couldn't quite get it out of her mind. She found herself eyeing Caneletto Cottage speculatively. Aunt Janetta had named all her cottages after artists and she had given her own name to her most special cottage. Caneletto Cottage stood the closest to the water and because of that, it had been everyone's favorite. The view from its front window, a miniature version of Aunt Janetta's own, was unforgettable.

Maybe, just maybe, I could fix up one cottage, Jenny thought slowly. Just the one. Caneletto, of course. Even if it's not perfect, the view makes up for a lot. I could rent it cheap, not perfect, the view makes up for a lot. I could rent it cheap, get a weekly income in the summer. Maybe by the month in winter for some skiers. It wouldn't be much, but it would get me by. What would it take? Some paint, a new fridge and stove, some curtains. If the mattresses aren't too musty. I wonder what condition the couch is in, she thought? And the chairs? Jenny jumped to her feet. I'll find out, she thought, right now!

Just then William came swinging down the beach from his uncle's place. "Hi there!" he called out cheerily.

"William! You're just in time. Come and help me figure out what to do with Caneletto Cottage!"

William frowned. "What do you mean?"

"I want to rent it out, just the one. I can't begin to fix up all six, at least not right away, but even one would give me an income, a small income, just enough. What do you think?"

Jenny was excited now, the words tripping over themselves as they spilled from her eager mouth.

William was cautious. "Well, it's an idea," he said. "You're going to look at it now? Why don't I go and get Uncle Wes?"

But Jenny was too impatient to wait. "We don't need Wes," she exclaimed. "Wait here, I'll go and get the keys!"

Jenny raced into the house and made straight for the shallow cupboard in the kitchen. Yes, it was just as she remembered: six nails, each with five or six keys, each neatly labelled. And there, on its own nail, was the master key ring. Jenny snatched it up and ran back outside. William was standing by the bench, looking doubtful

"I still think we should get Uncle Wes," he began, but Jenny interrupted him. "No, no, let's go right away," herding him toward Caneletto Cottage. "Now it's probably not going to be very good, but if only the roof hasn't leaked, or the pipes burst, or some other catastrophe, it should be possible to fix it up," she chattered, as she thrust the key in the lock. It turned easily. Jenny pushed the door open, still talking excitedly . . .

And stopped. Dead. Slowly, she looked around the cottage. She couldn't believe it! Fresh paint gleamed from every wall. In the kitchen, beside a modern coffee maker, stood a new stove and fridge. A comfortable couch stood against one wall. There were pretty curtains and scatter rugs on fresh, vinyl flooring. And was that a TV in the corner? Aunt Janetta never allowed TVs in her cottages! But it was. And under it was a VCR, with a shelf of videos just waiting to be played. There was even a hint of pot—pourri in the air.

Jenny's mind focused on this one insignificant point.

"Can you smell it?" she asked William. "Can you smell the pot-pourri?"

William looked confused. "Well, yeah, but . . ."

Suddenly William's sheepish look sank in. Jenny stared at him.

"You knew!" she said accusingly. "You knew this cottage was all fixed up!"

William shrugged. "Actually, they all are," he said hesitantly.

"What!?"

Jenny was electrified. Whirling, she raced out of the cottage. One by one, in a wild rush, she went to Titian Cottage, to Monet, to Carr, to Picasso and to Lautrec. It was the same story in each of them—fresh paint, new appliances, pretty furniture. And pot-pourri, in every damn one of them!

Bewildered, Jenny went looking for William. He had returned to the bench.

— 57 —

"All right, just what the hell is going on?" she demanded.

William shifted uneasily.

"Your aunt fixed them up," he said. "For you. So you'd have an income."

"What are you talking about?" Jenny's voice was rising. "Aunt Janetta didn't know I'd need an income. She didn't even know I'd be here! What do you mean she fixed them up for me?"

William sighed. Clearly he wished that someone else, preferably Wes, was here doing the explaining.

"Look, Jenny, just sit down, will you? I'll try to explain."

Unwillingly, Jenny sat down on the bench, but remained perched tensely on its very edge. She was wound tight as a spring.

"Jenny, for about six months before your aunt died, she was in a lot of pain. They prescribed morphine, but she didn't like to take it; it made her sleep all the time. She said if she only had a few months left, she didn't want to spend them sleeping!"

Jenny opened her mouth to protest. That's not the way it was!

William held up a hand to stop her.

"She didn't want you to know," he said. "She didn't want anyone to know, but she couldn't hide it from Uncle Wes, not with him over here three and four times a day.

"One day, she got this idea in her head. She said she knew you were going to come here to live and she said you'd need money. So she said she was going to fix up the cottages so they were ready to rent.

"It was a ridiculous idea. You were living in Mississauga, managing that art gallery; you seemed com-

— 58 —

her something to focus on. And Uncle Wes would have turned Janus into a retreat for penguins if he thought it would help Janetta through this. So he said he'd do the work. She wanted to hire our men, but Uncle Wes wouldn't hear of that. She only had her pension. He did all the work himself. And I helped, because I liked Janetta and because I didn't want Uncle Wes overdoing it. So we painted everything and laid new flooring and when Janetta said she wanted to refurnish them, too, we found a liquidation place in the city where she could get nice stuff at a fraction of its value. And, well, that's what happened."

Silence fell. Slowly, Jenny shook her head. "I can't believe it," she muttered.

William took a deep breath.

"Look, Jenny, your aunt wasn't some kind of magical gypsy fortune teller. It was a fantasy, even she knew that, I think; she was pretending, that's all. But it got her through the days. We had some happy times, the three of us, working in the cottages.

"But I don't think she ever thought it would actually happen. Uncle Wes and I certainly didn't! You could have knocked us over with a feather when you turned up here and decided to stay. It was almost spooky, like some kind of miracle."

Jenny shook her head.

"But weren't you guys going to tell me?" she asked plaintively.

Wes shrugged.

"Of course, Uncle Wes was just waiting for the right moment. He said you were a little upset about the box in the ground, he didn't want you to feel you were being led by the nose."

William eyed Jenny speculatively.

"So, are you mad?" he inquired.

"Mad?" Jenny looked incredulous. "How could I be mad when my aunt has just given me this incredible gift? And I don't know, but it did turn out the way she thought. Maybe it was just meant to be."

William looked relieved.

"Maybe," he agreed. "Anyway, however you look at it, you've pretty much got a turn-key operation here. You're in business!"

"Yeah," Jenny said thoughtfully. "All I need are some barbeques and a few Muskoka chairs."

William cleared his throat.

"Ummm, I think if you look if that old shed behind the garage you'll find some of that stuff."

"Really?"

"Yep, six new gas barbeques, twelve Muskoka chairs, six umbrella tables and six lounges. Janetta thought of everything!"

"Oh my God!" Suddenly, Jenny looked panic-stricken.

"But I can't do this! I don't know anything about running a cottage court. I can't have thirty-six people here all at once. It's crazy!"

William grinned.

"Sure you can. Calm down, Jenny, just think about it. You watched Janetta run this place all those years, so you must have picked a lot up. And you've been running your husband's gallery, you must know how to run a business. Just think, pretend you're giving advice to someone else. What would you say to do first?"

"Well," Jenny thought about it. "A business licence; that's first, I guess. And I should probably join the Chamber of

Commerce and put some brochures in their tourist office. And a website! Linked to the town's. Aunt Janetta already has e-mail, so I can direct inquiries there. And maybe a few ads in the Toronto papers, just because I'm so late getting started!

William grinned at the rising excitement in Jenny's voice.

"See? You do know what to do," he said approvingly. "Sounds like you're going to be busy."

Jenny laughed and jumped to her feet.

"You bet I am!" she declared. "Oh, wow, this is wonderful! You're right, I can do this. And I'll make it work, too."

William laughed, too. "Sure you will! Say, listen, Jenny do you want to go out to dinner tonight? To celebrate.

Jenny stared at him.

"Are you nuts?" she demanded. "I've got to get that brochure drawn up and start on the website. I've got to make plans, get things rolling! I can't go out for dinner!"

William groaned.

"Okay, okay, bad timing I guess. But, hey, this is Wednesday. By Saturday, you should have a handle on all this. What about Saturday night?"

Jenny looked at William as if she were seeing him for the first time.

"Well," she said consideringly. "Well, yes. Thank you. That would be very nice."

X

February 6, 1939

It is carnival time in Venice. And it has changed my life.
  Carnevale!
  Teresa is very clever with her needle and so she has made us costumes from remnants of silk and crushed velvet. Byron is an eastern potentate, most regal in his massive turban decorated with jewels — even if they are paste. They twinkle realistically! I am his harem girl, with navel exposed! It makes me feel very daring. And I will not even think of what Father would say.
  Though I have no jewels, I, too, twinkle realistically.
  John and George are dressed as ladies of the court. It shocked to me to see them put on such perfect femininity with their robes and makeup, but Byron has told me a secret. He told me they are homosexuals. I didn't know the word, and when Byron explained, I didn't know the concept either. I think I do not quite understand it even yet. What a silly, sheltered life I have led. But George and John are fine fellows and I do not care if they like each other best.
  Dorothea is a fantasy creature, utterly splendid in a feather

headdress three feet tall. It is made of peacock feathers, though I do not know where Teresa found such a thing. Teresa is Flora, all garlanded with flowers, and Ruth is a Viking with horns upon her helmet. How well it suits her! The men tease her, saying she looks no different than she does every day. Ruth just laughs, but they are right. She has that north wind look about her always. Pierre is a very sweet jester, with bells upon his many-cornered cap, and Paulo is a black knight with creaking armor. He takes pleasure, I think, in his cruel, spiked helmet.

And now it is the night we have designated for our carnival debut. For the past two or three days, we have been but spectators. Tonight, we will be participants!

We don our costumes and our masks and venture into the stone streets. The light from the street lamps casts eerie shadows. Paulo's spike becomes fearsome. We are not drunk, not yet, but I think we are intoxicated by the night, and by carnival. Venice itself makes us drunk! Ruth engages Paulo in a mock battle, club against lance, and Teresa is already scattering rose petals. She has a whole bag of them, but if she is not careful, they will soon be gone. Byron strides solemnly ahead, as befits a potentate, and I try to walk demurely in his wake. But that is not much fun, so I run ahead and take his hand. Perhaps he is an affectionate potentate! He must be, since he squeezes my hand with pleasure!

With much hilarity, we progress. Pierre is determined to play leapfrog with Paulo. I do not think it is a good idea, since Paulo will not remove his spike, but Pierre soars over his bulk as if the great knight were a mere hummock. Then he bends over and waggles his behind at Paulo, inviting him to take a turn. George and John make jokes about his posture that I do not understand, though I can tell they are very rude! Paulo is scowling furiously behind his mask because his armor is too heavy for such a jump. And then Teresa astonishes everyone by hiking up her floral gown and leaping high over Pierre. She flies through the air, landing nimbly, and we all applaud. All but Paulo, he is now in a passionate sulk, shown up by a mere slip of a girl! Well, he will get over it. And my goodness, Teresa's jump was grand!

In such a manner we make our way through the streets, playing and cavorting. We catch sight of other revellers, sometimes interacting with them, Pierre especially, continually playing leapfrog – with those not in heavy armor! John and George stay in character and I think no one guesses they are men. What fun! Byron has taken a horrible snake from his pouch and is pretending to charm it. It gives me quite a fright before I realize it is as fake as his jewels. And thank heaven for that!

At last we reach the Piazza de San Marco and at once we plunge into the milling throng. My heart is in my throat. What a spectacle! What pageantry! Here is Marie Antoinette, there is Pulcinello. Harlequins, pierrots, jesters, courtesans, angels and devils. There is Cassanova in all his splendor! Byron whispers to me that he is, in reality, an Italian count in love with the character, famous for his knowledge of Cassanova's life and loves. He has a different costume for each day of Carnival – but they are all of Cassanova. His jewels are real, I am sure of it! For once there are more people than pigeons in the square. Vendors hawk hot chestnuts, jugglers and mime artists perform, a lute player can hardly be heard over the shouts of the crowd, but his hat on the ground is filling with coins anyway. I am in love with Venice! With Carnival! It is surely the greatest event in the world.

There is no hope of meeting "under the Chinaman" tonight. Florian's is bursting at the seams, but Byron cleverly snags us a table in the outdoor loggia and we gather closely around it. Byron boldly changes my order and when the waiter leaves, he scolds me. This is not a night for cappuccino, he says grandly.

He orders me a Campari and soda, though I do not know if I will like it. But I will drink it because Byron ordered it just for me!

In fact, I do like it! Its tart freshness spills down my throat and I revel in its alien taste. This is sophistication! Why is that so important to me? Who knows? I shrug, I drink three of them quite rapidly and my head begins to spin. Pleasantly.

Now we are off again. Byron has wangled us invitations to a grand ball. He says we are to arrive in style and ushers us all into two gondolas at the pier. It is my first gondola ride and I wish I had space to enjoy the water singing under the prow, the lights shimmering on the water. But all is hilarity, silliness. In no time we arrive at the palazzo, its private dock a blaze of light. We disembark, among many other boats and guests and Byron disappears for a moment. I see him talking to a gondolier on the other side of the dock and I am momentarily curious. But he quickly returns and in the excitement of entering the palazzo, I forget my curiosity.

We sweep into the palace, safe behind our masks. Indeed, I do not think I would dare to enter such a grand edifice otherwise. But my mask hides little Janetta Canal from Canada in comfortable anonymity. I could be anyone in this mask, a countess, a princess, a beautiful courtesan. We make our way up the stairs to the piano nobile and enter the ballroom. I gasp at the sight. The room is lit by thousands of blazing candles, sparkling everywhere, casting a glow of enchantment on the costumed guests. At once our small party disperses. I am left with Byron who holds my hand tightly.

We drift across the ballroom and come across a sumptuous buffet. Platters of lobster and shrimp are piled high, caviar stands about in small dishes. A waiter in a white coat is dismembering a huge turkey. Out of its cavity comes a duck, I cannot believe my eyes. Out of the duck comes a quail and out of the quail comes some other small bird, a cornish hen perhaps. This seems almost decadent. All those dead birds! But then I catch sight of something that pleases me more. It is a huge swan, carved out of ice. What skill has gone into it! Every feather stands out, its eyes glitter. All that artistry for something that will simply melt away! But for this moment, it stands, a splendid creation.

Beauty is always ephemeral.

This room is like nothing I have ever seen. It is the size of a hockey rink, though that is an inelegant comparison. But after all, I am Canadian; such a comparison is second nature to me! Rich damask draperies adorn the tall windows and the ceiling is painted. How glorious! Surely that fresco, the one in the middle, is by Tiepolo! Could it be? In a private home? But this is a very ancient private home, the seat of nobility, Byron tells me, so I suppose it might very well be. Amazing. How could you live with a ceiling by Tiepolo? How could you live up to such achievement?

A chamber orchestra is playing Vienna waltzes on a dias at one end of the room. Fabulously costumed creatures are sweeping grandly about the dance floor. But slowly, as my eyes become accustomed to the candlelight, I become aware of a contrast, a puzzling paradox, almost a pantomime of good and evil. In the centre of the room, on the dance floor, all is elegance and beauty. But in the shadows, the corners, some very odd things are happening. A man has a young woman pressed against the wall, his pants open, her dress rucked high. Another man vomits openly into a potted palm. I recoil from the shadows, try to focus on the gaiety of the centre of the room. Perhaps that is the problem with such opulence. And perhaps that is the problem with these wonderful masks! They make constraints disappear. All hint of propriety vanishes.

I lift my chin. I am here to enjoy myself, not to compose an essay on licentiousness! I take Byron's hand and he whirls me onto the dance floor. This is better. Here, all is splendor, all is enchantment. I will not dwell on the shadows. Or in them.

Several hours pass. We dance, we eat a light supper — imagine a supper of caviar! — we stroll on the terrace above the Grand Canal. We catch glimpses of the others in our party, but we do not connect with them. And then Byron takes me by the hand and leads me out of the palazzo.

I am disappointed. Must we leave? Already? But Byron is whispering that he has a surprise for me. I like surprises. He leads me to the gondolier he was speaking to earlier and explains. He has hired a special gondola for three hours. We will see all Venice by night, just the two of us! I squeal with pleasure. What an excellent surprise!

But what is a special gondola? Soon I see. It is a gondola with a kind of cab or box in the middle. I remember that Caneletto painted many of them, but they have since vanished from Venice. I don't know why. They are very sensible and give privacy and protection from the elements. But I suppose most gondolas are now given over to tourists and they only ride in good weather. This gondola has been specially rigged for Carnevale. I can see that the cab can be easily removed for more normal duties. What fun this is going to be!

The gondolier, in his striped shirt and ribboned hat, lights a torch at the prow of the boat. A real torch, with a live flame. Already I can feel the romance of this excursion creeping over me. As we settle in the cabin, the romance swells. We are half reclining on fur. Perhaps it is some ratty old coat of squirrel that would not stand the light of day but here and now, it is delightful luxury. There are fresh roses in a vase fastened to the wall and there is an ice bucket, with a bottle of champagne and two crystal glasses. Byron has thought of everything.

We push off into the night. To my astonishment, the gondolier immediately begins to sing, some passionate Italian number. I giggle with embarrassment. But then I remind myself not to be so, so Canadian, and I give myself up to the moment.

It is magic. We drift in the darkness as the mist swirls up from the dank waters of the canal, whirling in the flames of the torch. The gondolier's rich tenor calls out across the water and is answered, faintly, by gondoliers on other boats, other missions. The lights from the passing palazzos make lacy patterns on the dark, secret water that carries us so softly, so gently. We drink several glasses of champagne, we snuggle into the fur, we revel in this dark, mysterious parade. How odd to think that back in the ballroom people are still dancing, still eating caviar. Here, time has fled. It is as if we glide alone through a strange, watery world.

And then Byron kisses me. At once I feel an answering surge of — of what? This is all new to me. Something urgent, compelling. Can this be passion? I do not know, but I am clinging to Byron, calling out as he loosens my clothing, touches me. I tremble with pleasure as his mouth finds my breasts, as his hand parts my legs. The boat rocks, the gondolier sings louder, and my eyes fasten on the torch over Byron's shoulder as it flames and flares. In the distance, carnival fireworks fill the air, their cannons thudding through me.

And so Byron and I became lovers. I was virgin, foolishly innocent, but Byron taught me all I needed to know. I was a very willing pupil! And afterwards, he held me tenderly, gently, as if I were a precious piece of Murano glass, and he whispered that he loved me.

Byron loves me.

And nothing will ever be the same.

XI

"Janus was the god of harbors."
– New Larousse Encyclopedia of Mythology

It was Saturday night. Janus was soon to be a member of the Wasaga Beach Chamber of Commerce. Jenny had applied for a business licence. The brochure was being printed. The website was in the works—Jenny had been looking through her aunt's many photograph albums, picking out the best shots of the beach and the garden. It would be a great website!

William had taken her to the nicest restaurant in town, a seafood place, and they had feasted on fresh oysters and some kind of Tex-Mex shrimp dish. Spicy, but delicious! Conversation had flowed easily, though there had been one surprise: Jenny had found out that Uncle Wes wasn't really William's uncle at all!

"He and my Dad were best friends," William explained. "I grew up calling him Uncle Wes. I was at this big architectural firm in the city and not very happy, no chance of any hands-on work there! So, when Uncle Wes offered this job, I jumped at it. I was only going to stay in the house for a few weeks until I got settled, but we got along so well and Uncle Wes isn't as young as he used to be. I can be of some help to him. So, I stayed. It's worked out quite well."

Now Jenny and Wes were enjoying an after-dinner stroll on the beach boardwalk at the busy, commercial end of Wasaga Beach. The sunset was fiery, the Blue Mountains just a purple smudge in the distance. Jenny was recounting odds and ends of Wasaga Beach history she remembered from stories Aunt Janetta used to tell her.

"The very first overseas flight from Canada took off from Wasaga Beach," she was saying.

"You're kidding." William sounded surprised. "Wasaga Beach doesn't even have an airport, does it?"

"No," Jenny replied. "But it was interesting. This was back in the 1930s and all the airplanes then were very small. So, if they were going to make it across the Atlantic, they were going to have to strap extra fuel tanks on. They could do that, but the problem was the extra tanks made the planes heavy and they needed an extra long runway to take off. Therefore, they came to Wasaga Beach where the beach was a natural runway. It fit with the history of the place, anyway, because the beach was the first road here. For years. They didn't ban cars from the beach until 1974. These guys were aiming for Baghdad to set a long-distance flying record, but they were forced to land in England — but it was still the first overseas flight from Canada."

"Funny place to try it from, though," William said. "Why fly over half a continent? You'd think they'd start from the coast."

Jenny laughed. "There was an earlier flight from Newfoundland," she admitted. "But Newfoundland wasn't part of Canada until 1949. So the flight that took off from here was the first overseas flight from Canada."

They continued to stroll in companionable silence. Suddenly Jenny laughed again.

"Aunt Janetta used to say that Wasaga Beach must be the only town in Canada that named its main street after a lunatic," she recalled. "There was a guy called James Mosley, a hermit, and not very social He lived in a shack in the woods, hunted and fished for a living. But the solitude got to him over the years. He got more and more peculiar and finally went completely crazy. But Aunt Janetta always said the great thing about Wasaga Beach was that it let people be. It was kind to its eccentrics. She said she knew that because she was one herself—though not as crazy as James Mosley!"

William laughed and Jenny thought how pleasant this was, just strolling along, chatting with a friend. William was a friend, she realized. A good one. At some point, he had taken her hand and Jenny found she liked that. Quite a bit, in fact.

Suddenly she remembered something.

"Oh," she exclaimed. "I've been meaning to ask you. When that idiot Thornton was talking to Wes, he said something about you building a street. Wes said that was a special project. What did he mean? How do you build a street?"

William's eyes lit up.

"Uncle Wes was right. It's my baby," he said. "I had this idea and Uncle Wes said go ahead, try it. What a terrific guy he is! Anyway, the idea was to build the perfect family street. You know, something different than rows and rows of boring boxes."

"What do you mean?" Jenny asked curiously.

William stopped. "Do you want to go and see? There's enough light left. I'd like you to see it."

Surprised, Jenny agreed. They were soon in William's truck, heading south of the river. He turned into a street and jumped out of the truck. Jenny joined him and they began to walk.

"First, I built the street in a crescent so there'd be no traffic except for those who lived on that street. I figured with everybody having kids, no traffic was important." William was talking rapidly now, engrossed in what he was saying.

"Then I didn't build any houses in the centre of the crescent; that was the stickler. A lot of money disappeared with houses just on one side of the street. But I wanted to make the centre of the crescent into a kind of village green. And here it is," he said proudly, waving his hand.

And, indeed, Jenny could see at once that this was something special. In the centre stood an adventure playground that looked extremely creative. Ropes to swing on and tunnels to crawl through. Its main feature was a wooden ship with a crow's nest and a curving slide swooping down from it.

"It's wonderful!" Jenny exclaimed. "And just look at all the flowers!" There were geraniums everywhere. Thousands of them, pink, white, red. William grinned.

"Janetta told me geraniums need the least amount of water," he said. "I didn't want maintenance to turn into a big issue, so that's what I planted."

Jenny nodded. "She told me that, too," she said, thinking of her clay pots. Elsewhere on the green was a basketball court, a shallow wading pool and a pavilion for block parties with picnic tables and built-in charcoal barbeques.

"This is great!" Jenny said. "What a perfect place for kids to play!"

"Yeah, and the nice thing is that people can sit on their own verandas and watch the kids in the park," William said. "It's good for everyone."

For the first time, Jenny noticed that every house on the

other side of the street had its own veranda. They had a good feel to them. People would get to know their neighbors, sitting out on the front porch, Jenny thought. Then she noticed something else. Every house was different. Some were wood, some brick, some stone, some had miniature turrets, others skylights. Each house was an individual statement.

"They're all different!" Jenny exclaimed.

William nodded.

"Who wants to live in a house that's just like everyone else's?" he said. "I wanted to give people lots of choice, so they could decide for themselves. Here, come into this one."

Willingly, Jenny let herself be guided across the street and into one of the houses. Inside she could see the care and attention to detail. A working fireplace was in the living room and the windows featured deep, padded window seats for people to sit and dream in. There was little luxury, for William had tried to keep the price down, but the rooms were spacious with small, imaginative touches. It looked like the perfect family house. A house to be happy in.

"I like it," Jenny said, turning to William. He was right behind her and she bumped into his chest. Almost of their own volition, his arms went around her.

"I'm glad you like it," he murmured. "I want you to think well of me."

Suddenly, without warning, his mouth came down on her's. The kiss was a long one, Jenny didn't know how long, somehow she lost track of time. But she did know that she liked it. A lot. William shifted and now Jenny could feel his manhood pressing into her. She felt an answering thrill deep within her own body. Slowly, William lifted his lips from her's.

"What do you say?" he asked softly.

Jenny leaned back in William's arms and looked at him. Suddenly she knew she was going to do this. It just felt right.

"I say yes," she said.

"But not here. Let's go back to Janus. That's where we belong."

❦

Next morning, Jenny lay in bed, more asleep than awake. Mostly she was aware of an extraordinary sense of well-being that seemed to have overtaken her in the night.

God, I feel good, she thought sleepily. She had no idea why, but then the thought of William came into her mind. William! Of course. Jenny snuggled deeper under the duvet.

Jenny had never been a big fan of sex. It was okay, she had always thought, but secretly she had never understood all the fuss. But then, she'd never been with any man but Bram.

Now, now she had been with William. And now she had a different tale to tell — not that she'd be telling anyone, that was for sure! But William had been a whole new experience for her, at once tender and urgent. And powerful, so powerful, thrusting deep within her, making her come again and again. Welcome to the world of multiple orgasms, she thought dreamily. And what a world it was.

Happily, she reached out for William. Maybe we could do it again, she thought daringly. But her hand encountered only empty space. Jenny's eyes flew open. Disappointed, she saw William was gone.

At once, all the old Bram-type insecurities came flooding back. He didn't want to face me, she thought. He probably regrets the whole thing. Hurt and miserable, Jenny was about to dive back under the covers — possibly forever — when she heard a strange noise. It sounded like someone was sawing. Mystified, Jenny got out of bed and pulled on a short, terrycloth robe. When she walked out onto the front verandah, she stopped in surprise. William was there, dressed only in jeans, no shirt, no shoes, and he was sawing a big hole in the verandah floor. For a moment, she was so happy to see him, she didn't even care about the hole. But curiosity overcame that.

"William! What are you doing?" she exclaimed.

William looked up and saw her. He jumped to his feet and Jenny couldn't help admiring his well-muscled chest, the set of his broad shoulders. He came close and kissed her.

"Good morning, sweetheart," he said cheerfully. "I'm building us a hot-tub."

For a moment, all Jenny heard was the endearment. He called me sweetheart, she thought happily. Then the rest of it sunk in.

"You're building a WHAT?"

William grinned. "A hot-tub," he repeated. "It'll be great. Just the two of us, late at night, looking at the lights over the bay, soaking in the hot water. Scent. Bubbles. Sensuous delights."

William was laughing, but Jenny could only sputter.

"I've never been in a hot-tub in my entire life," she declared. "And I certainly can't afford one. I think . . ."

William placed one finger across her lips.

"Shhh," he said. "Don't fuss, Jenny. Listen, when I woke up this morning, I felt so . . . so splendid . . . that I knew I had to find some way to say thank you. And then I thought of putting in a hot-tub. It's a gift. I know you'll like it! Please,

Jenny, say it's okay."

Jenny looked at the gaping hole in the veranda floor. "It's a bit late to be asking permission," she laughed. "But, yes, of course it's okay! It's a wonderful surprise. Thank you."

William gave a shout of pleasure, then folded her into a massive hug. "There's just one thing," he said, laughing. "This is a no-bathing-suits-allowed hot-tub."

Jenny emerged breathless from the hug. She lifted an eyebrow.

"I can live with that," she said.

XII

March 3, 1939

For a month now, I have written of nothing but Byron — how he touches me, how he makes love, what fun we have in my small bed under the eaves, how I have painted his wonderful profile over and over again — and still have not got it quite right. But I am here to study art, not love, and in fact I am learning a great deal. So, I will write about that for a change!

Most nights, Byron and I have dinner at a trattoria just down the street. (It didn't take me long to get back to Byron, did it?) But it is a wonderful restaurant. The owner has a soft spot for art students. He will often trade a meal for a painting and the walls of the trattoria are bursting with them. Paintings everywhere, squeezed into the smallest corner. It is very effective — and a very long way from the lone painting over the parlor sofa that is the norm in Toronto. How boring that is! We should fill our walls with art!

Over supper, we mostly talk of painting and often we are joined by the others. (We talk of love later in the evening, when we are alone.) But Byron has helped me to understand things, his technical knowledge is greater than mine. (Though I dare to think that maybe, just possibly, my painting is as good. But in any case, our styles are very different.)

Byron also helped me to overcome my shock and embarrassment after our first "life" session. I did not know what that meant, I thought we would be drawing flowers or fruit. (Well, they are alive!) But you can picture my astonishment when a man strode into the classroom, took off his robe and posed there, stark naked! I didn't know where to look! There were lots of giggles and titters, but our drawing master cut them off sharply and proceeded to give us a long lecture on the basics of art.

"We start here," he said. "With the human form. If you can't draw it, you can draw nothing. We will draw bones, we will draw muscles, we will draw flesh over bone and muscle. This is not a naked person in front of you; it is pure form. And it is a form you must conquer!"

And, you know, he was right! In no time I was caught up in the flow of my pencil and quite forgot I was looking at a naked man — the first I had ever seen! (Besides Byron, of course.) Drawing him became merely a project. Indeed, I became quite blase about nudity, and rightly so — it is form and shape, that is all!

One mistake I made at first is that I expected all the models to be beautiful. But very few of them are; instead, they are fat, they are old, they are ugly.

"Beauty, pah!" our drawing master sneers dismissively. "Anyone can draw a pretty picture! Here, we draw LIFE!"

He is severe, our drawing master. But a very good teacher. Every day I can feel myself coming closer and closer to the essence of art. If only he would let us paint! But no, it is draw, draw, draw! I have filled five thick sketchpads already. And used up dozens of 2B pencils. He says we will not be ready to paint until we can draw in our sleep. It is infuriating. But, you know, I think he may be right. Everywhere I look now, I am seeing form and contrast, lines, angles. A plate of spaghetti is not a plate of spaghetti to me any more; it is an interesting collection of curves and lines. I think of everything in terms of how I would draw it. Perhaps that is what he wants!

It is odd. Caneletto is perhaps Venice's most famous painter — and yet there are none of his paintings here. Perhaps one or two. But by far the majority of them were sold to well-to-do English tourists and I suppose they rest there, in England, in stately homes and crumbling castles, a touch of the exotic among the roast beef and hunting dogs. I have an excellent book of Caneletto's paintings and I study it constantly. He was what was known as a "view painter" and his great strength was perspective — even though he often re-arranged buildings to make the view more pleasing! His other great strength was atmosphere: you don't look at his paintings, you feel them! If I can achieve only that in my own paintings, I will be happy.

For although I am not allowed to paint in school, I paint all the time. All weekend and every night after dinner. Byron spends all his time in my room now and he has moved his easel in, so we spend long evenings painting together. Sometimes we create still lifes as an exercise and each paint our own version of the same thing. It is great fun: a candle, a book, a rose, perhaps a bottle of wine. And how different the two paintings turn out to be! Byron is a superb technician, his renditions are very faithful. And very beautiful — you'd swear you could bite into his apples. My own paintings are different. I like to stretch shapes, add bold strokes of unexpected color. Byron teases me, saying no one will buy a blue apple. I would!

Do you know what? This is a secret. I have posed nude for Byron, many times in fact. I must say his faithful renditions *here make me a little nervous — if Father ever saw even a single one of these nudes, he would know at once it is me. And I would be dead! But I cannot say no when Byron wants to paint me. He makes me beautiful. He makes love to me with his eyes as he works. And the paintings arouse both of us — hardly is that last brush stroke taken when Byron approaches me. And I am at once lost, shameless, perhaps even wanton.*

He brings me such joy!

Our little band has been reduced by one. Paulo disappeared in the night. He is not missed. I don't know what happened, but the day after we went to the ball in Carnival, Teresa appeared with a black eye. She would not speak of it, just pressed her lips together in a thin, hard line. But Paulo was gone all that day and that night he packed up and left without a word of goodbye. Byron was very angry, I know, and so was I. I am sure he hit her! Poor Teresa. Her Carnevale was not as pleasant as mine! Now, though, she has become friends with Pierre, and he is very sweet and gentle with her. She seems happy.

Ruth has not met anyone but she, too, seems happy. She actually found a rowboat somewhere and rows everywhere in it. She has given me several rides. It is not a gondola, that is for certain, but it is good fun. She snorts when I say that. "It is good exercise," she corrects me.

"Yes, of course," I laugh. And Ruth smiles, puzzled.

It is Dorothea who has astonished us all. She is dating a count! The one who dresses as Cassanova, whom she met during Carnival. I think it is madness; he could hardly advertise his penchant for infidelity more clearly. But Dorothea says it is just for fun. I hope she remembers that, I would not like to see her hurt.

I wish I could capture more fully the flavor of my days here in Venice. Here, in this place, every day is adventure. But they are adventures of the moment, of daily life. Small things. But wonderful! Fresh-baked bread, a rough Chianti, pungent cheese. Byron's hands upon me. Drawing, always drawing. Laughing with Dorothea. And riding the vaporettos for hours, drinking in the golden light of Venice, its shapes and stones.

I love Byron so much!

And I am so very lucky.

XIII

April 1, 1939

Byron is gone.
 Gone!
 And I am bereft. I cry, I wail, I beat my fists upon his empty pillow. But he is still gone. Already I miss him so much!
 And I am frightened for him. He has gone to England to join the air force. He says there will be war, so he must be ready.
 "But you do not know how to fly!" I scream at him. He only laughs, says he will learn. "If you love me, you will not go," I weep. But Byron takes my hands, talks to me seriously. "It is because I love you that I must go," he said. "I must do my little part to make the world safe for loves like our's."
 It is not little to me. No one's love is like our's. It is not safe. HOW CAN HE LEAVE ME????
 I was so angry at him. But I could not bear to say goodbye in that way. So I pulled myself together and organized a gay party at the trattoria for him, everyone gathering to say goodbye, even the drawing master looked in to wish him luck. We made love all that night, not for a moment did we sleep. We

talked and cried and laughed and made love over and over. How tight he held me! "Never think that I want to leave you. And never doubt that when this war is over, I will come to Canada and find you. And we will be together forever."

Canada. No matter how brief this war is, that is where I shall be. Father has written to say I must come home at once. He, too, thinks there will be war. He says it is too dangerous to stay, even in Venice with all my friends. He says Mussolini is a dangerous man, that anything might happen. He has booked my passage for me, in just three days' time. I dare not disobey him.

All this leaving. Byron has left me, and now I must leave Venice.

I cheer myself by thinking how dashing Byron will look with a white silk scarf wound round his neck.

Or rather, I try.

XIV

April 15, 1939

Byron is dead!
 Byron is dead!
 Byron is dead!
 No matter how many times I write it, I cannot believe it. How CAN he be dead? Byron was my life. And now that he is dead, how can I continue with life? Life is nothing now, meaningless! I have no life, just as I have no Byron.
 It is so silly, so ridiculous and pathetic. He was going to do such great things, fight this war, then come home and marry me, give me children, live as an artist. He would have been a great artist, I know. He had such plans, such dreams!
 And instead, he never even got started. Not for one moment did he fight. It was his first training flight. Something went very wrong, the plane caught fire, it went down in flames into the English Channel. My beautiful Byron, so handsome, so alive, burnt into nothing! Dead! And for what? For nothing, nothing at all. I cannot bear to think of the pain and the fear of it.

Byron had talked of me. Often. And so they sent me a cable telling me of his death. I stood in the doorway of the pensione, reading it over and over. I could not make sense of it! Byron, dead? No! Impossible!

I did not know I was screaming until Dorothea tore the cable from my hands and read it. Everyone gathered. They gave me brandy. I cried and cried and cried until I was numb. I could not even think of catching this boat, I wanted to stay in Venice, visit and re-visit all the places where Byron and I had been happy.

But my friends said I must. My father was expecting me. It would do me good to get away from Venice. I could do nothing, I could not. I lay on my bed, hot tears burning my face. I screamed to think of Byron's noble profile, burned and charred beyond recognition. But Dorothea washed and dressed me, Teresa and Ruth packed my bags. Pierre and the boys from New York carried my luggage to the harbor. The drawing master turned up at the ship.

"Now you must live for your art," he said. I turned away from his stern face, suddenly so kind. I only wanted to live for Byron.

Now I have been at sea for many days. I have no more tears to cry. Over and over I have stood at the rail, thinking to hurl myself over, to join Byron in that cold, salty grave. I longed for the oblivion it offered.

But in the end, I didn't. Because Byron, I know, would want me to live! He would say I must go on, live for both of us. And on the other side of the ocean, my father awaits. I cannot give him the kind of grief I bear. So no, I will not kill myself. I will live on.

Even though my life is over.

XV

"Janus was the god of private doors."
– New Larousse Encyclopedia of Mythology

Jenny closed the journal carefully and stared into the fire.

So, that was the story! Such pain. And how terrible for Aunt Janetta to be so much in love, on the brink of a wonderful life—and to have it all torn away in a moment. A cable arrives and, just like that, your life is over!

No wonder she had never married. Jenny had never understood that. Aunt Janetta had been beautiful, full of fun, lively. Plenty of men must have been interested. But, clearly, she had loved Byron all her life, Byron, and no other.

Still, she had gone on. She must have felt her life was over. She had made a new life, here at Janus. She had painted, she had gardened, she had been kind to a niece.

But she had never loved again.

"How brave you were," Jenny whispered.

XVI

"Janus was the head of all human enterprises."
– New Larousse Encyclopedia of Mythology

"What about the toilet seat?"

Jenny stared at the woman blankly.

"Uh, what about it?" she finally replied.

"Well, should we bring our own?"

Good grief! With an effort Jenny kept a straight face. It was the beginning of June and she was holding an open house at Janus for all prospective summer visitors. It was going very well but, my goodness, she was getting some odd questions!

In another moment, though, all became clear. Funny how there was always some logic to even the looniest questions. In this case, the woman had rented a cottage somewhere the year before, had been faced with cracked toilet seat and, finding that uncomfortable, had purchased her own. Now she seemed to be wondering if she should routinely bring it along whenever she rented a cottage.

Jenny assured the woman that the toilet seats at Janus had no cracks in them, and she happily booked a cottage for the second week in August. Great! Almost full, Jenny thought with satisfaction. Her future at Janus was secure—

and bless Aunt Janetta for that, she thought fervently.

Just then William approached the small table Jenny had set up on the deck to take bookings. He had volunteered for duty today and had been a great help, handing out lemonade and answering endless questions about the garden and the fish. Now Jenny grinned as he came up the steps.

"I told you the play garden would be a hit!" she called out.

William had been wonderfully supportive, even building a smaller version of his adventure playground for the courtyard, but he had laughed at Jenny's idea for a play garden. She had nailed pots of flowers to brightly painted sleds and wagons and then had painted a sign on a big, foot-shaped patio stone inviting children to take the flowers for a walk. William had predicted the flowers would sit, unmoving, but at this very moment, Jenny could see six little kids industriously hauling the flowers all over the courtyard. The idea was mysteriously popular with three and four-year-olds.

"The great thing is the play garden will look different every day, depending on where the kids leave the flowers," she added, as William sat down beside her.

"Okay, okay, you were right. You obviously have a child's mind," William joked.

"Hey!" Jenny laughed as she ruffled William's hair, then gave him a quick hug. God, she was happy! This was working! All her ideas, the herb garden for guests to pick their own fresh chives and parsley, the play garden, the special sunset benches, the marshmallow roasts she planned twice a week—all seemed popular with the guests. She'd be busy as hell all summer, but she'd be busy right here, at Janus, just where she wanted to be. And her money worries were over.

Just then, another woman approached.

"Are these cottages sound-proof?" she asked.

Jenny assumed she was worried about noise from the other cottages.

"Janus is a family place," she hastened to explain. "We don't allow any rowdies or all-night parties."

But apparently the woman had something quite different in mind.

"Oh, I'm not worried about that," she said. "It's just that I can't stand the noise of the waves."

Jenny was flabbergasted. Why holiday at a beach if you didn't like the sound of the waves?

"I really think you'd be happier somewhere else," she said firmly.

William looked at her in surprise as the woman walked away.

"If she shut the windows and the doors," he began, but Jenny shook her head.

"All we'd need is one night when the bay was rough and she'd be miserable," she said. "And I've decided I only want happy people here at Janus," she added seriously.

William laughed.

"Great business decision," he said.

Jenny grinned.

"Okay, it'll never happen," she said. "But I want to start out that way at least."

Just then another woman came steaming up to the deck, a sour look on her face. Jenny looked at her doubtfully. She was pretty sure she didn't want her at Janus either.

"Your website is very misleading," the woman announced.

Jenny felt herself bristling. Stay calm, stay pleasant, she

reminded herself.

"Actually, I don't think it is," she said. "What seems to be the problem?"

"You have pictures of roses on the website—and I don't see a single rose here today!" the woman said triumphantly.

Jenny decided the woman must live in a condo in downtown Toronto. Certainly, she didn't know anything about gardening!

"It's the first week of June. The roses come later."

"Oh." For a moment, the woman seemed taken aback. But she was determined to complain about something.

"Well, you don't offer much here anyway," she sniffed. "You don't even have a swimming pool!"

Astonished, Jenny glanced at the big, beautiful bay right in front of her—possibly the biggest swimming pool in the world! But there was no point in saying that. This woman was determined to be unhappy.

"You're right, we don't," she said briefly, before turning to the next woman. To hell with Mrs. Steamroller! Fortunately, the next woman was a very different sort.

"Miss Canal, I just want you to know that my family and I think Janus is charming," she said. "The beach, the gardens, the playground, the artwork, all the extra little touches—I have a feeling, now that we've found you, we'll be coming back for years,"

Jenny beamed. This was more like it. Happily, she began to search her register for a week this nice woman could book.

William slipped away to replenish the lemonade. "Don't forget you're coming for supper tonight," he whispered. "Just come on over when you're through here."

Jenny smiled.

"You bet!" she said.

XVII

"The name Janus evokes the idea of the luminous sky."
– New Larousse Encyclopedia of Mythology

Jenny was walking the last of her guests, a friendly, older couple, out to their car. To her surprise, they had introduced themselves ten minutes ago, saying they used to stay at Janus in the old days when Aunt Janetta ran the place. They were delighted Janus was re-opening and booked two separate weeks for the summer.

Now, as they walked through the garden, the woman suddenly laughed.

"Still painting the allium, I see," she said.

"You know about that?" Jenny asked, grinning.

The woman laughed again.

"Well, I didn't. I was as fooled as everyone else," she explained. "Then I came out of our cottage early one morning and caught your aunt spray-painting them. I thought at first I must be mistaken, that it was a weed treatment or something, but no, she was actually painting the flowers!

"We had quite a laugh over it. I never told anyone, even though it was pretty tempting!"

Jenny laughed and bid the couple goodbye, then headed back to the house to comb her hair, put on some fresh lipstick. What a great day! Her summer season was now full and she had even picked up a few bookings for the fall. You're in business, kiddo, she told her reflection. Then she headed next door.

When she got there, William was fussing with the barbeque.

"You're having dinner tonight at the home of two bachelors," he announced. "And that means steaks!"

"Sounds good to me," Jenny replied.

"Why don't you go on inside and rustle up Uncle Wes?" William said. "Tell him there's a thirsty man about to cook for him. He might want to keep me happy. You can have a drink, too," he said with mock generosity.

Jenny laughed and headed inside. When she got to the door of the living room, she paused. There was no light on in the room and Wes stood at the window, head angled to look down the beach. With light pouring in through the window from outside, Wes was backlit. Jenny couldn't see his face at all, just his silhouette.

Jenny caught her breath. In this light, all the familiar signs of age had fallen away. She couldn't see the wrinkles or the scars, not even the whiskers. All she could see was his profile.

It was the most beautiful profile she'd ever seen. She thought of her aunt's diary. And suddenly, she knew.

She gasped.

"You . . . you . . . you're Byron!"

XVIII

"Janus was supposed to have invented navigation."
– New Larousse Encyclopedia of Mythology

Wes switched a lamp on and suddenly the illusion vanished. Now there was just a nice old man standing in front of her. But Jenny knew what she had seen.

"You are Byron, aren't you?" she asked. "But you can't be! He died, his plane crashed . . ."

"I wondered if you'd catch on," Wes said. He chuckled. "Yes, I'm Byron, damn fool nickname that it was. And as you can see, I'm not dead yet!"

Jenny was reeling. She felt light-headed.

"I don't understand," she said simply. "Please tell me."

"It's a long story," he said. "I guess we'd better put those steaks on hold." He called to William and a moment later all three were in the living room. Wes poured wine for each of them. He took a deep breath.

"It was like this," he said finally. "I didn't die in that plane crash. Not quite. It was a near thing. I was badly burned, pretty busted up from the crash, too. But there was a life preserver in the cockpit and I managed to grab it, hook it over one arm. And then I just floated. I was unconscious some of the time from the pain. It was bad. I lost track of time. Then, a day later, maybe two, a German boat picked me up more dead than alive."

Jenny stared at Wes, aghast. All alone in the icy English Channel, burned, injured.

"I was lucky," Wes continued. "None of us were hardened to death yet. A year later they would have shot me just for fun. But this was early on. They picked me up. there was a doctor on board. He was an enemy, but he saved my life — I've never forgotten that. I spent the whole goddamn war in a prison camp. Lot of help I was, eh?"

Wes shook his head and a tiny silence fell. Jenny broke it.

"You tried," she said. "That's all anyone could do. But what happened after that? You were going to marry my aunt, live as an artist. What happened?"

"What happened?" Wes laughed harshly. He held up his gnarled hands. "This is what happened. I broke my hands, most of my fingers in the crash. The doctor was trying to keep me alive; he didn't worry much about my hands, never set them. They didn't heal right. When the war was over, I took stock. Didn't like what I saw. I was a handsome lad once, but no more. My face was scarred. I was a monster. And my hands were ruined. I couldn't even pick up a brush, much less paint a picture. My life was over."

Wes shrugged.

"I was useless. I couldn't lumber your aunt with that. She thought I was dead. I figured it was best to stay dead."

Suddenly Wes looked fierce.

"I wanted her to be happy. And I knew she couldn't be happy with me, not any more. So I went back to Toronto — maybe you didn't know this, but your aunt and I grew up in the same neighborhood. We were friends. It wasn't till we got to Venice that we fell in love.

Wes shifted in his chair.

"I went back to Toronto, but not to the old neighborhood. I didn't get in touch with Janetta. I took a room near Jarvis Street and set out to drink myself to death."

"What?" Jenny was shocked. Wes nodded.

"I wasn't thinking straight. I figured my life was over — I was just putting in time. I never slept rough, though, never used those hostels and soup kitchens. There was always something I could do, wash dishes, shovel snow. I made just enough to pay for my room and my bottles and I told myself that was enough. Mostly I just drank."

William leaned forward. He was shaken.

"But you're here," he protested. "In this great house right on the beach, you've got a wonderful business and you're a famous carver. What the hell happened?"

Wes laughed, an oddly tender laugh.

"Janetta happened," he said. "A few years went by and one day I was sitting on a bench with a few of my drinking buddies. We were passing a bottle in a brown paper bag back and forth. And suddenly I looked up and saw Janetta staring at me." Wes glanced away.

"I never thought I'd see her on Jarvis Street. But she'd come down there to visit someone in the hospital. And she recognized me! That's what I could never get over. With the scars, the beard, the lousy clothes, she still recognized me!"

"And so you got together," Jenny sighed. "A happy ending."

Wes laughed again.

"It wasn't quite like that," he said dryly. "When I saw Janetta staring at me, I just lost it. I didn't want her to see me like that. I ran away, just plain ran away. I can still hear her calling after me. But I lost myself in the crowd, ran back to my room. Opened a new bottle."

"Ohhh, no!" Jenny breathed.

"Oh, yes. But, you know, your aunt was a determined lady. She tackled my buddies. They never had a chance against her. She found out where I lived and a couple of hours later she turned up at my room. She stood in that doorway, looking at the room. It was dirty, threadbare. It smelled. I was pretty drunk by then. 'Go away,' I slurred. 'I'm dead, remember?' But Janetta wasn't standing for that. She bundled me into her car, didn't pack a thing, just drove away with me incoherent in the back seat and came right here. There was just her house and a bunch of bush then, no cottages, no garden. She put me to bed to sleep it off. When I came to in the morning, she was waiting with breakfast — bacon, eggs, fresh juice. I hadn't had that kind of food in years. I ate everything in sight. But the whole time I was thinking that right after breakfast I'd leave, hitch-hike back to the city, maybe move on to Montreal where I'd never be found. I was dead and I didn't want to come back to life. I had nothing to live for. But your aunt, darn her, had burned my clothes. Here I am acting out this damn tragedy and your aunt comes on like it's a comedy. Burned everything! And she laughed when I got mad. There were no stores here then and I could hardly hitch-hike in my underwear. So I had to stay. She hid all the wine. For a few days I just ate and slept. I gradually healed. For the first time, I really began to heal. Your aunt looked so fine, like an angel, I couldn't think we'd get back together. But I was still young and strong, the booze hadn't had time to finish me, and as I ate and didn't drink and rested in that heaven of clean sheets and sweet-smelling rooms, I began to feel pretty good. Then, one day, she put a hammer in my hand. 'Build me a cottage,' She said. 'If I'm going to keep this house, I have to have a cottage I can rent. I need the money.' At first I protested, said I didn't know how. But she knew that wasn't strictly true. I'd worked summers on my father's construction crew for years. And I knew I owed her. So I said I'd build the damn cottage and then leave. She said fine. Your aunt was a smart lady. I guess she knew what would happen. You see, at first I thought I'd just throw up any kind of shack and get on my way. But I got kind of interested in it. And my father never ever allowed shoddy work. I began feeling better every day. So I built Caneletto Cottage and I did a pretty good job—all these years later, it's still standing. And somehow, as I worked away with all that fresh wood and paint, I lost the urge to drink. I lost the urge to leave. I built the best damn cottage I could and then gave it to Janetta. It was the only gift I could give her. And you know what? She loved it! She carried on and on about how great it was. I felt kinda proud. She came into my arms to say thank you. I kissed her and it was like all the years fell away and we were back in Venice. She didn't care about my scars, not at all. The next morning, I knew I wasn't going anywhere. I'd been given a second chance and, by God, I wasn't going to waste it!"

Jenny was wide-eyed, William still as a stone. No one spoke. Wes grinned a little self-consciously.

"It took awhile. Janetta lent me the money to buy a pickup. I started a little business, not building houses, I wasn't confident enough for that, not yet, but I built porches and spare rooms and garages and put on new roofs. I paid her back in just a few months and in about a year I had enough saved to buy a lot. That's when I built my first house. It sold fast, almost as soon as I finished it, and that was the start of

GG Construction—from Byron's name, George Gordon. By that time, we could laugh about that Byron business. And I just kept building houses and selling them, eventually hiring a guy to help, then a couple more. In my spare time, I built the rest of her cottages. And when this land came up for sale, I grabbed it—what a chance, to live next to Janetta!"

The old man fell silent for a moment, lost in memories.

"We had a good life together," he said finally. "Your aunt gave me my life back. Even the carving. About a year after my first house, she put something else into my hand, just like that first hammer. This time it was a chisel. Carve me a Janus head, she said. You might not be able to paint any more, but you can use a hammer and chisel. And you know what? She was right. I didn't have the use of my hands, not for fine work, but I still had my eye and my sense of design and I found I loved carving. And, like I said, your aunt was smart—that creative part, that was the one thing missing. When I got that back, I was whole again. I set out to give Janetta the best life I could. Just before she died, she told me I'd succeeded and then some. Made me real happy."

Jenny swallowed hard. She was deeply moved. But one thing puzzled her.

"Why did you stay here, next door, for so many years?" she asked. "Why didn't you two marry, like you'd planned."

Wes eyed Jenny speculatively for a long moment.

"I'm praying Janetta won't get mad when she hears this," he said. "But I figure it's time you knew. Above anything else, even me, you were important to Janetta. You came first. She figured as a maiden aunt, she could stay closer to you.

Wes took a deep breath.

"You see, honey, Janetta was your mother."

XIX

"Chaos took on the form of Janus: his two faces represented the confusion of his original state."
– New Larousse Encyclopedia of Mythology

Jenny was stunned.

She was sure she'd heard wrong. Right? She must have! "Could you repeat that?" she asked carefully. She felt sick to her stomach. All these secrets!

"You are Janetta's daughter," Wes said firmly. "And you better believe she loved you!"

But before Jenny could react, William had sprung to his feet and come to stand over her protectively.

"That's enough!" he shouted at Wes. "Are you crazy? You can't spring this kind of thing on her. It's too much. She's had a good day, a great day. The first, maybe, in a long time. For Christ's sake, let her enjoy it!"

But Jenny was shaking her head.

"No, William, I have to hear this," she said. "Wes is only doing what he thinks is right. And I agree. This is something I have to know. Please go on, Wes."

Glowering, William threw himself back into his chair. He wasn't mad at his uncle. Not really. How could he be? But he was worried about Jenny. She was white as a sheet, and she was trembling.

"Please, Wes," she prompted him.

Casting a worried look at William, Wes continued.

"All those years in the camp and on Jarvis Street, I was a damn fool," he said. "I was all wrapped up in my own troubles. I pictured Janetta with some other guy, totally happy, our time in Venice forgotten. And I thought it best to leave it forgotten. But it wasn't like that. Janetta was lost without me, I should have realized. I knew what we meant to each other. Anyway, she went into her own tailspin. She didn't end up on Jarvis Street, not her, but she did date some unsuitable men. And one of them got her drunk, did his thing, and left her pregnant."

Jenny felt suddenly cold. Freezing.

"You have to understand. Things were different then. Nice girls didn't get pregnant. And if they did, it was hushed up. Janetta had no money. Not a cent. She loved you so much, Jenny, even before you were born. But she knew she couldn't keep you. Her father was beside himself. But he loved Janetta and he tried to work out what was best. By then Janetta's brother and his wife had been married three years and no kids had come along. They had just found out she was barren. It was quite a blow. Janetta's father arranged for her brother and his wife to adopt you. Janetta had to promise never to tell you, never to interfere. They didn't want her to have anything to do with you, but Janetta held out for aunt. She would be your aunt under the law, she said, and it would look funny if she didn't act like one. But really, she just wanted to stay close to you, be close to you. She had you three days and then they took you away. Janetta was devastated. Her father bought her the house on the beach, figured that would distract her, and get her out of town, let his son and his wife settle in with the baby."

Wes paused.

"It all worked out pretty well. Janetta began to work out her life here. You had a loving mother and father — and a loving aunt. When they saw Janetta meant to keep her end of the bargain, they softened, let her take you for the summer. I would have loved to marry Janetta, adopt you. You'd have been a wonderful daughter. But I was drinking myself silly on Jarvis Street the whole time Janetta was going through this. I've never forgiven myself for that. But that's the way it was. And when we got back together, Janetta had made up her mind never to marry. Anyone. Not even me. We had a good life together, anyway. And as a single aunt, she knew it would seem natural for her to take an interest in you. You have no idea what those summers meant to her. She loved every second of them. And as her art career and the cottage court began to go well, she sent money to your father all the time for clothes and toys and for school. She paid your tuition at art school. When your parents died, she thought about telling you. But she didn't want to upset you. She decided things were best left as they were. But Jenny, my dear, your mother loved you. Never doubt that for a moment."

Jenny sat perfectly still. Memories washed over her. So many things were clear now. The extra toys, the pretty dresses, the money for art school. Of course, she had known even then, though vaguely, that her father couldn't afford such things. But, like any kid, she hadn't given it much thought. And all those summers! She closed her eyes and against the shut lids she could see Aunt Janetta and herself walking hand-in-hand along the beach, watching the sunset, talking. And laughing. Always laughing.

Jenny opened her eyes and saw Wes and William watching her anxiously, identical expressions of concern on their faces.

Suddenly Jenny felt wonderful, completely and absolutely wonderful.

She'd loved her parents, always would, but she had loved Aunt Janetta, too; there had been a special connection there. And now it was validated! Janetta Canal—that wild, slightly eccentric artist, gardener extraordinaire, that liver and lover of life—had been her true mother! Had watched over her. She hadn't been a mistake, something to be forgotten as soon as possible. She had been central to Janetta Canal's life. Always and forever.

Jenny began to smile and almost laughed at the relief that came over the faces of the two men before her.

"I guess I'm lucky," she said finally. "I had three wonderful parents. I was loved."

ଔ

It was late. Wes had gone to bed and Jenny and William stood on the porch, William's arm tight around her shoulder. They had finally eaten the steaks. All night long, Wes had talked of Janetta, it was if a dam had burst. Story after story. And Jenny had hung on every word, loving him, loving her aunt—no, her mother! Her mother had done her best for her, Jenny had no doubts about that. And she loved her even more knowing that.

"All these secrets," Jenny sighed now to William. "It's not a very profound statement—but you just never know what will happen, do you?"

"No." William held her close. "Listen, Jenny, just one more secret, ok? One more, and then we'll never have another secret between us."

Jenny leaned back to look into William's face.

"What now?" she asked, nervously.

William laughed.

"Just this," he said huskily. "I love you, Jenny, and I want us to spend the rest of our lives together."

Suddenly, Jenny laughed joyously.

"That's not a secret!" she exclaimed. "That's a promise! And here's another one."

Jenny looked deep into William's eyes.

"I love you, too," she said.

XX

Jenny and William sat in Florian's, under the Chinaman painted by Pascuti in 1858. Before them sat delicate cups of cappuccino, sprinkled with cinnamon, and slices of rich, dark chocolate cake. Jenny reached across the table to take William's hand.

"This is a dream come true," she said happily. "Venice, Florian's, the two of us here together!"

William squeezed her hand. He looked just as happy. "Thanks to Uncle Wes," he said.

It was late September. Summer, now come and gone, had been a lively, bustling success at Janus. Jenny hadn't quite succeeded in only having happy people there, but the problems had been few and easily solved. It had been a great summer, more than half the guests had already booked for next year. The future of Janus – and Jenny – looked good.

And then, as they were sliding thankfully into autumn, Wes had sprung his surprise. Two plane tickets to Venice, reservations at La Calcina, Ruskin's Hotel, right on the Guidecca Canal, Janetta's old stamping grounds, just steps from the Academia. They had arrived the night before and now Jenny was almost bursting with happiness.

First, the gondola ride, the water slipping softly under its prow. And yes, the gondolier had sung for them. And then the Piazza de San Marco, with its pigeons, its campanile, and most of all, the great, gilded cathedral. They had gone through the cathedral, rode to the top of the campanile, wandered around the shops in the loggia — Jenny was still sighing over a life-size tree of blown glass with leaves and parrots, all glass. The ducal palace they had reserved for tomorrow. But now, now, they were in Florian's, in the very place where Janetta had sat so often with her Byron. It was a cycle, a continuing, life — affirming cycle, she decided.

Jenny raised her cup.

"To Janetta and Byron," she said softly.

And remembering the loving words in an old calfskin journal, they drank.

ca

Back in Wasaga Beach, Wes lit a fire, poured himself a glass of wine. Then he settled himself in front of the fire, lighting a huge, Cuban cigar with a sigh of satisfaction. Their pleasures had long been forbidden to him, but now it didn't matter. The time had come.

Wes had been fighting the pains in his chest, along his left arm, for months. First, to be there for Janetta, then to see Jenny safely settled. Now that everything was done, the will leaving everything to William made, he'd decided he wasn't going to fight any more. He had spent the night before writing letters to William and Jenny. Then this morning he had worked for a few hours, for the very last time, in Janetta's garden. Now it was time.

He'd gotten them safely off to Venice, out of the way.

He'd made his arrangements. By the time they got back from Venice, glowing and more in love than ever he'd bet, he'd be safely buried. They could visit his grave, sure, even bring flowers, but there'd be no death watch, no panic, no grief. Well, maybe a little grief, he hoped so anyway, but they wouldn't have to deal with his death. It would all be over. William would be furious, but that Jenny, she'd soon soothe him, settle him down.

Wonderful girl, Jenny. A wonderful daughter. Made a man proud. He'd thought about it, over and over, and in the end decided she had the right to know. No more secrets. Hell, he'd have told her that night, the night she realized he was Byron, if William hadn't gotten so mad. But finding out Janetta had been her mother, maybe that had been enough for one night. And so he'd written the letter, telling her at last of his love for her, his pride in her.

But imagine them thinking Janetta had slept with some drifter! It had been all he could think of on the spur of the moment. But she only slept with me, he thought with a flicker of pride and ownership. Even now. It was his fault it hadn't worked out. What a damn fool he'd been to marry that floozy in a drunken lark. It had been in his Jarvis Street days and she'd only hung around for a week or two, then vanished. He'd been glad to see her go. But he'd been sick with anger when Janetta had become pregnant and he couldn't marry her — because he was already married.

They had talked about it. Endlessly. Live together. Go away and pretend they were married. But every option seemed tainted with dishonesty. Things were different then, just like he'd told Jenny. They couldn't just live together, not if they wanted to give Jenny a respectable life. And they had no money, then. He was just starting, had just bought that first old truck, Janetta was struggling to keep Janus. And there was Janetta's sister-in-law longing for a baby, her brother, a good man, wanting one too. It was the right decision, Janetta had said. They can do so much more for her. He had wept the night Janetta had decided, but she had made up her mind.

Well, it had all worked out.

Wes felt the pains begin deep in his chest. He put out the cigar carefully. No point burning the place down. He sipped his wine as the pains grew stronger. He was tired of fighting; it was time to move on.

When the hammer blow came, he cried out, just once. The room around him grew dim, replaced by a blinding, white light. And yes! There in the light was Janetta, holding out her arms to him. She was young again, pretty as a picture.

And the handsome young man with the curly hair and the beautiful profile ran to her, lifted her high in the air, then held her close. His lips found her's.

They were together again.

ଌ

The sun was setting and its dying rays caught the gilt of the cathedral, sending it into a blaze, a fire in the sky.

Jenny and William had finished their cappuccino and now stood in the piazza. Jenny was breathless with awe.

"The light!" she cried. "Look at the light!"

William drew her to him, buried his hands in her hair. "It's our light," he whispered. "Our time in the sun."

And then he, too, kissed the woman he loved.

There were no more secrets.